The hairs on Carmen's neck stood up.

Footsteps sounded behind her. Then a hand clapped over her mouth and nose, cutting off her breath.

For a second, panic rose in her chest. Her mind slipped back to the attack twelve years ago... No. She couldn't allow herself to go there. To feel weak and vulnerable again.

"Can't you take a hint?" the voice growled near her ear.

Ignoring the ache in her lungs, she jabbed her elbow into his gut and spun to face him. Her mind registered the ski mask...and the voice. Familiar but not quite, a blast from the long-forgotten past. She swung out her arm, her keys sticking out from her fist.

The man screamed in pain, clutching his eye and taking off.

New footsteps came close. Jonah.

"S-someone tried to kill me," she breathed.

"The same person who chased you at the lake?"

She shook her head. And that's when the realization hit hard—more than one person wanted her dead.

Jaycee Bullard was born and raised in the great state of Minnesota, the fourth child in a family of five. Growing up, she loved to read, especially books by Astrid Lindgren and Georgette Heyer. In the ten years since graduating with a degree in classical languages, she has worked as a paralegal and an office manager, before finally finding her true calling as a preschool Montessori teacher and as a writer of romantic suspense.

Books by Jaycee Bullard

Love Inspired Suspense

Framed for Christmas
Fatal Ranch Reunion
Rescue on the Run
Cold Case Contraband

Visit the Author Profile page at LoveInspired.com.

COLD CASE CONTRABAND

JAYCEE BULLARD

LOVE INSPIRED SUSPENSE

INSPIRATIONAL ROMANCE

LOVE INSPIRED® SUSPENSE
INSPIRATIONAL ROMANCE

ISBN-13: 978-1-335-58857-9

Recycling programs
for this product may
not exist in your area.

Cold Case Contraband

This is a work of fiction. Names, characters, places and incidents are either the
product of the author's imagination or are used fictitiously. Any resemblance
to actual persons, living or dead, businesses, companies, events or locales is
entirely coincidental.

For questions and comments about the quality of this book, please contact us
at CustomerService@Harlequin.com.

Love Inspired
22 Adelaide St. West, 41st Floor
Toronto, Ontario M5H 4E3, Canada
www.LoveInspired.com

Printed in U.S.A.

To appoint unto them that mourn in Zion, to give
unto them beauty for ashes, the oil of joy for mourning,
the garment of praise for the spirit of heaviness;
that they might be called trees of righteousness,
the planting of the Lord, that he might be glorified.
—*Isaiah* 61:3

In gratitude to God for my family's two newest littles, Adeline Ann and Samuel Johnson.

And to my super reader brother Nate—
thank you for always reading my books and
giving such kind and thoughtful comments.

ONE

It would be ten years ago this December since Sara Larssen's body was found floating in the water less than twenty yards from the spot where Carmen Hollis was currently standing. Carmen had been two thousand miles away when the news broke, a sophomore at UCLA, with not enough cash to fly home for the funeral. So she had fired up her computer and tried to find anything she could relating to the murder of her favorite teacher and friend.

She had learned very little in those early days of searching. News reports revealed that Sara had been beaten before she was drowned and left for dead, and that particular piece of information had struck a chord with Carmen, bringing up memories she had been working hard to forget. But as the years passed, no suspect was arrested, and no motive was revealed. The murder of Sara Larssen became just a dead-end case getting colder by the day.

Which begged the question of why Carmen had chosen this bright autumn morning to visit the scene of the decade-old homicide. Did she really think that she, the newest and youngest member of the Foggy Falls police force, would find something that so many before her had missed? Investigators had already spent hours combing through the evidence, interviewing neighbors and analyzing every aspect of the case. All she had to offer was a fresh set of eyes and a resolute desire to bring a killer to justice.

She had parked her car in a lot on the west side of Isla, one of the smaller of a chain of lakes off the coast of Lake Superior. She clipped a leash on her foster pup, Bruno, and then set off for a stroll along the shore.

Her gaze flickered past a half dozen docks jutting into the water, stopping on the weather-beaten plank with faded black painted numerals marking Sara's lakeside address. There had been plenty of pictures of the crime scene in the case file, but she pulled out her phone and snapped a few more, tilting her cell for a wide angle of the compact, almost circular little lake. The piney scent of the cool north woods filled her lungs as she watched the waves form tiny ripples against the rocky beach. This was what she had missed when she lived in LA. Crystal clear water. Clean, fresh air. The brilliant reds and spun gold of the elms and maples. The quiet beauty of God's creation.

And the happy splash of a walleye doing belly flops in the middle of the lake.

The morning sun was warm on Carmen's face as she walked up the trail, past the battered Adirondack chairs positioned for a view of the water and the dilapidated "little free library" on the edge of the property, which Sara used to keep stocked with books for neighbors looking for something to read.

Bruno pulled on his tether, desperate to check out all the good smells up ahead. She had been working hard to train the little pup to return at her whistle, so she reached down and unclipped his leash so he could roam. On the far side of the trail, a gray squirrel scampered through a patchwork of fallen leaves as the snap of twigs hinted of something larger approaching through the trees.

Animal or human?

The answer came a second too late as the barrel of a gun pressed against the small of her back.

Fear coiled in her gut as a deep growl curled against her ear. "Set down your weapon and phone and put your hands on your head."

A man, then. Young, or youngish, judging by the timbre of his voice. And by the faint scent of artificially woodsy body spray, like the kind her stepbrother used as an all-purpose cologne and deodorant.

Her fingers lingered inches from her shoulder harness, itching to disobey. Years of experience with the LAPD had taught her that it was a mistake to forfeit her weapon. Sweat beaded on her brow as she willed her mind to stay sharp and focused.

"Any sudden move, and I'll shoot." The man pressed his gun harder against her back. "Do as I say, and no one gets hurt."

Yeah, right. Not likely.

But her options were limited. It would be best to wait until he made a mistake.

Reaching deep into her jacket pocket, she pulled out her cell. Then she slipped her Sig out of the holster and set it next to her phone on the ground.

"I know the person who lives here. Sara Larssen? I was hoping to surprise her with a visit."

"Yeah. Well, that might be a problem because she's dead. But I'm thinking maybe you knew that already. What do you say we move closer to the dock, and I'll show you where it happened?" Using his weapon as a prod, he nudged her down the trail toward the lake.

Her glance skirted toward the clearing where Bruno was watching the ducks on the beach. Pulling in a deep breath, she let out a low whistle.

The head of the short-haired pup swiveled to attention. He was a smart dog, and she knew he was always hoping for the chance of a game.

"Time to play," she said, leaping aside as nine pounds of muscle and fur careened into the gunman's chest. His gun flew out of his hand and into the air, landing on the ground just a few feet away. She tried to grab for it, but the man's leg shot out, kicking her feet out from under her and knocking her into the dirt. As her assailant scrambled to claim his fallen pistol, Bruno leaped through the tangle of arms and legs, knocking the gun even farther from her reach.

"Get out of here, you stupid mutt." The man drew a knife from the pocket of his pants and swiped it through the air.

Bruno yelped and scurried out of the way.

Now! This was her chance! Carmen bounded upright and jammed the top of her head into the soft cartilage of her assailant's nose.

"Why you…" A torrent of expletives flowed

from his lips as blood gushed down the front of his shirt.

Carmen dived for the weapon. She would've had it, too, if the man's long fingers hadn't locked on her arm, wrenching it away. Suddenly reenergized, Bruno leaped back into the fray, clamping down hard on his wrist.

With the gunman's screams ringing in her ears, Carmen scooped the puppy into her arms and sprinted toward the trees.

Jonah Drake banked the Cessna low along the horizon, his eyes scanning the white foam churned up on the water by the November wind. Soon the ice would begin to form on the lake, and the shipping activity along Superior would close for the season. An overwhelming sense of disappointment niggled at the edge of his mind. If things didn't go well, this could be his last case as an investigator. True, he had been initially hesitant to return to undercover work after four years working a desk at the headquarters of the Bureau of Criminal Apprehension in the Twin Cities. But after three months on the job, he was finally getting close to uncovering the source of the drugs being peddled to teens at Foggy Falls High.

Glancing down at his watch, he saw it was

nine thirty. Betty would be awake by now, excited by his promise to take her to the zoo today. His mother-in-law was always willing to cover for him, but he was determined not to take advantage. Elizabeth had already uprooted her life to accompany them to Foggy Falls, and though she loved Betty as much as he did, even a doting grandmother deserved a break from being the full-time caretaker to a lively four-year-old.

He shifted his focus to the sky outside the cockpit window. Visibility was excellent, with the sun already high on the horizon. He'd make one more pass by the smaller inland lakes along Superior's western shore and then call it a day.

It was hard to shake his growing frustration. An anonymous source had claimed that a delivery of fentanyl was scheduled to take place along the lakeshore today, and he was determined to check it out. Far too many innocent lives had been lost to the deadly drugs that had been pouring into the area. A different time, a different place, and it could have been the story of his brother Jerrod's addiction and death.

But thus far he had seen nothing to prove the tip's veracity. Had his intel been wrong? Or had he missed something in his initial

recon of the area? A large freighter had an-
chored offshore in the early hours of the
morning, and if there were drugs on board,
the contraband would have to be unloaded
sometime soon. But in a half dozen passes
near the freighter, he hadn't noticed anything
amiss. He studied the water again, hoping to
catch a glimpse of a bobber, a flag, anything
to suggest a rendezvous point with a smaller
vessel. But only the icy blue-gray expanse of
Lake Superior greeted his gaze.

A flicker of movement caught his eye.
He leaned forward for a better view. Something—or someone—was running along the
trail that hugged the shoreline of Lake Isla.
His eyes shot to the altimeter. He was already
flying low, and if he dropped down much
lower, he would alert whoever was out there.
It might be just an innocent civilian out for a
jog. But it was the only break he'd gotten so
far. He pushed forward, edging the nose of
the Cessna down and around.

The black dot appeared larger. Whoever it
was seemed in quite a hurry. The figure was
moving at a breakneck pace, weaving a hap-
hazard route along the rugged trail. Probably
not a jogger then. Most runners stuck to the
path between the lakes and avoided the shoreline. But it was impossible to tell exactly what

was happening down there on the ground. Had the noise of the approaching airplane spooked the runner, or was something more sinister going on down there?

A moment later, the figure—a woman, on closer inspection, who appeared to be clutching something in her arms—changed direction, diving to the left as a second person appeared behind her, gaining in pursuit. There was clearly some sort of chase taking place. He needed to take a closer look.

He pulled up on the throttle and turned the Cessna in the opposite direction. Then he nosed down again. At the lower altitude, he could see a gleam of metal reflected in the second person's hand.

The hairs on the back of his neck stood up. Did the scene unfolding on the ground below have something to do with the drugs being offloaded from the freighter? He couldn't be sure. And in the long run, it didn't matter.

Because if he didn't intervene, he could become a witness to a murder.

He had two options, neither one ideal. He could land the plane and try to rescue the woman being pursued, or he could attempt to distract the individual with the gun. But getting involved at this point could cause him to lose the only lead he'd had in the case. And landing the plane on the choppy water presented its own challenges and left him and the rented Cessna vulnerable.

It was a hard call, but he made his decision.

His hand shifted to his waist and flipped the snap of his holster. And then he took a deep breath, before pushing down on the throttle and the elevator.

Carmen's lungs ached as she sprinted along the trail. Her tactical training had kicked in, so instead of making a straight beeline for the stand of pines, she was weaving side to side, even as gunfire echoed through the air. But Bruno was a deadweight in her arms, slowing her pace and affecting her balance. She needed to double back toward the lot where she parked her car, but the man behind her seemed to sense which way she was heading and kept trying to push her off course. And it was working. She jerked her body in the opposite direction again, her legs pumping fast.

At the roar of a low-flying airplane, a new sense of dread snaked down her back. The small, two-seater Cessna was less than fifty feet from the ground and looked like it was on the verge of landing. Was the pilot in league with the shooter on the ground? She couldn't allow her mind to dwell on that possibility.

Her eyes darted to the left and right, and the thin bubble of hope she had been holding on to burst. She was essentially trapped.

To her right, the stand of trees was already thinning, giving way to the shore of Lake Superior. Could she risk a dive into the frigid water?

She looked down at her clothes. Black jeans, a flannel button-down shirt and a bulky coat. If she jumped into the lake, she'd have to shed the jacket to avoid getting pulled down by its weight. And the water would be freezing this time of year. Even though the ice hadn't solidified yet, she could see frozen chunks below the surface.

Her heart throbbed a staccato beat in her chest as a bullet buzzed through the air.

She shifted her trajectory. Her legs felt leaden, and her assailant was getting closer, his footsteps thrashing through the dry grass behind her.

And the rumbling from the plane in the air above her was getting louder.

The Cessna, which had looked so small as it cruised above her, now loomed enormous just a few feet over her head. The din from the engines was deafening. She watched in a kind of horrified fascination, her body still moving forward but her gaze frozen on the aircraft as it descended. A cascade of water sloshed up behind it as the plane's skis made contact with open water, and the Cessna taxied away from her in the opposite direction, slowing down.

Relief surged through her senses. But half a second later, that strange giddiness was doused by fresh dread as the plane executed a neat U-turn toward the spot where she was headed.

She cast another peek behind her. The shooter was still advancing. She sent up a whispered prayer. *Please, God! Save me! If anything happens to me, who will be around to help Kirby?*

An image of her stepbrother flashed through her mind—his crazy haircut and the permanent surly expression plastered on his face. He had been five when she left town, still a towhead, always with a book in hand, destined to be the brainy kid in a family of jocks. But things had changed a lot since then. Kirby was no longer that adorable little boy who curled up on her lap and begged for a story. The teen had been arrested twice for possession and was currently on court probation.

Her senses amped up to high alert at the ear-piercing whistle of another bullet streaking through the air. She scrambled to make sense of what was happening. That gunshot had come from the opposite direction. Her eyes skirted toward the aircraft to the sight of the pilot hanging out the window, pointing a pistol in her direction. Her body tensed as three more shots exploded through the air. Realization dawned, and she took off sprinting. The pilot was aiming at the man behind her and providing her cover to cross the last twenty feet of the path to the lake.

Dashing the remaining distance while holding Bruno tight in her arms, she sprang up and made a flying leap into the plane.

Jonah didn't wait for his passenger to settle into her seat before jamming the throttle. He needed to get the plane back up in the air ASAP. Without any cover, they were essentially sitting ducks, and if a stray bullet hit the gas line, well…best not to think about that. He could feel the water churning beneath the skis as they gained speed, but a glance out the side window showed that they weren't safe yet.

Pop! Pop! Crack. A bullet splintered against the glass. His body jerked to the side as a hiss of wind found entrance through a bullet hole, and immediately a web of disjointed lines crisscrossed the shattered windshield. He glanced down to check his speed. A wave of relief washed over him as he pulled down on the yoke and felt the nose of the plane pull upward. In just a few minutes, they would reach the proper altitude, and he could level the aircraft.

He handed the woman a headset that matched his own and then waited for her to adjust the ear pads and microphone.

"You okay?" he asked.

She shot a glance sideways, her brown eyes catching and holding his. "I think so. But I don't know about Bruno."

"Bruno?" It took him a second to realize that she was talking about the squirming puppy on her lap. A compact little dog looked up at him through wide eyes and then snarled through a set of small, pointed teeth.

"My foster pup. He's usually more polite. But he got a pretty bad cut on his right leg. Do you have anything I can use to stop the bleeding?"

The first aid kit on this type of Cessna was usually stored in a small compartment above the controls. Jonah reached up and flicked open the lid and then handed the inside container to his passenger.

She rifled through the contents, piling several items on her lap. Jonah watched out of the corner of his eye as she tore open an alcohol swab, pressed it against the wound, then used a swatch of gauze to wrap the pup's injured leg.

"Thanks," she said, pushing the box back into the overhead compartment. "That ought to do for the time being."

Jonah nodded, hiding his unease. Something didn't quite add up here. Though the woman was clearly worried about her dog, she was acting way too calm considering she had barely escaped an attempt on her life. Why wasn't she panicking? Was stress causing her to shut down her normal reactions?

He aimed to find out.

"Glad the kit was reasonably intact. You never know with these rental planes. Name's Jonah Drake, by the way."

"Carmen Hollis." She offered him a weak smile. "Thank you for saving my life. I'm so sorry about the damage to the plane. When we land, I'll give you my contact information so I can cover the cost of repairs."

Carmen Hollis. He repeated the name in his head and then added a quick description. About five foot six, with a smattering of freckles and eyes that matched her chestnut brown hair. She was pretty, very pretty actually, but not in an overly fussy kind of way.

There was something natural and straightforward about her smile.

"We don't need to worry about any of that at the moment." He pointed toward the two-way radio under the instrument panel. "Why don't I call 911 and report the incident?"

"Thanks. But actually, I'm an officer with the Foggy Falls Police Department. Before I file a report, I'd like to talk to my chief and find out how he wants to proceed on this."

A cop? He wasn't expecting that. Was it true? He shook his head. "But if you don't do anything, the shooter is going to get away."

Carmen's brow furrowed, her expression reluctant. "Possibly. You're just going to need to trust me on this."

Trust her? He had been trained to *distrust* everything and everyone, to question any and all assertions that didn't make sense. His shoulders tensed as Carmen dug her right hand into the inner pocket of her jacket, but then relaxed as she flipped open a wallet containing her badge.

He gave it a quick scan. It looked authentic. But he had been warned about a possible leak within the local police force. Was it a coincidence that this particular incident had taken place near a drop spot that was part of his investigation?

But any follow-up questions would have to wait. They were closing in on the Duluth airport, and he took a wide arc as he began his approach. As he prepared for landing, he sneaked one final glance at Carmen Hollis of the Foggy Falls Police Department, a mysterious cop with a suspicious agenda. He definitely needed to do a little more digging into why his path and hers had crossed in such a dramatic way.

TWO

It took ten minutes of haggling, but the operations manager finally agreed to a twenty-four-hour reprieve in reporting the damage to the plane.

"I'll fill out the forms tomorrow," Jonah promised, backing out the door of the small Quonset hut adjacent to the main hangar. Worried that the man might change his mind, he hurried across the asphalt path toward the spot where Carmen stood waiting, her expression strained as she cradled her dog in her arms.

"Let me give you a ride home. It only makes sense since we're headed in the same direction. I just need to check in with my mother-in-law and let her and my daughter know I'm on my way home."

He pulled out his cell and called her. Liz answered on the second ring. "Hi, it's me. I'm just now leaving the airport. I'm going to miss lunch, but I should be home in an hour, tops. But we may need to postpone the zoo trip to another day."

"No worries," his mother-in-law said. "We'll see you when you get home.'" He ended the connection and turned to face Carmen. "That's my car over there," he said, pointing to a blue Subaru Forester at the edge of the lot.

This couldn't have worked out better if he had it planned. The drive back to town would present a good opportunity to learn more about Carmen's so-called case.

When they reached the Subaru, Jonah waited for his passenger to climb inside, settle the pup on her lap and snap on her seat belt before he pulled out of the lot and headed north toward Foggy Falls.

"Off we go," he said. "How's Bruno doing?"

She looked down at the little dog. "Much better. Still sound asleep."

"My daughter has been begging for a pet. But it just doesn't seem feasible since she won't be the one taking care of it."

"You could always foster a pup like Bruno. It's a good way to see if a pet fits in with your family. How old is your daughter?"

"Four and a half. Almost five, actually."

"That's such a fun age. I remember pestering my mom for weeks to let me bring home the hamster at preschool. She didn't go for it either. What's her name?"

"Betty," he said. "She's named for her grandmother."

"I like it. I didn't even ask if you live in town, or are you just up for the weekend?"

"I teach Spanish at the high school. We recently moved from the Twin Cities, so this place has been quite a change."

"I hear you. Small town versus big city. I grew up here, but I've spent the last twelve years in LA. Talk about an adjustment. I traded in warm weather and five-lane highways for dirt roads and freezing cold. Is your wife a teacher, too?"

"Um." He hesitated, not really wanting to answer. He dreaded the usual lame platitudes and pitying looks he got in response, but there was no polite way to avoid such a direct question. "My wife died almost five years ago. Right after my daughter was born."

Her expression softened. "I'm sorry. That must have been tough. Probably still is."

"Thanks. We're doing okay, though."

As he negotiated the turn onto Highway 61, he glanced through his rearview mirror at the black Jeep Grand Cherokee that had slipped behind them for a moment before drifting back out of sight. It was the same make and model of a car they had passed earlier in the airport parking lot. He tapped the brakes and waited for the driver to get close enough to allow him to see the front plate.

But the vehicle hovered stubbornly out of his field of vision.

"How about you? Do you have family in the area?" Jonah's eyes remained fixed on the mirror, waiting for the Jeep to reappear behind them.

"At this point, it's pretty much just my mom and stepdad. And my stepbrother, Kirby." Carmen paused. For a moment, Jonah thought she was going to say something more. But instead, she turned sideways and stared out the window at the wind-tossed waves crashing against the shore.

He couldn't blame her for preferring the scenery to the conversation. Did the people who lived around here ever get used to the spectacular view? The gray-blue sky provided a perfect backdrop to the deep navy water and the pale pink and speckled brown rocks along the coast. In the past week, the leaves on the trees had come into peak color, and the traffic on the two-lane highway that snaked north from Duluth to Grand Marais had become thick with tourists, crowding the small towns along North Shore.

Jonah pushed his tortoiseshell frames against his nose and did another quick check in the mirror. An SUV pulling a trailer had edged into the space behind him. It appeared they had left the Jeep in the dust. Good. Maybe the suspicion that they were being followed was just in his imagination.

He dug through his limited fund of small talk, scrambling to make conversation. His interrogation skills had gotten rusty after so many years working the desk at the BCA.

Still, he remembered the basics. The idea would be to start with some general questions about the weather and then work his way back around to asking about her job and the case she was working. "So," he said at last. "I heard someone say it's going to be a cold winter."

Carmen tore her eyes away from the view and swung around to face him. "I sure hope not. I've lost any skills I once had for driving in the snow and ice."

"It's not so bad if you take your time. But I suppose in your line of work, that's not always an option."

Carmen smiled, and he was struck again by how pretty she was. Pretty, but focused.

An interesting combination. He didn't usually notice those things, nor had he been drawn to anyone this quickly since his wife had passed. But there was something about the woman sitting next to him in the passenger seat that jolted him out of his usual haze.

They were getting closer to their destination, and he still hadn't made any progress in finding out what Carmen had been doing before she encountered the shooter on the trail by the lake.

"Is your car nearby?" he asked. "Or do you need a ride to retrieve it?"

"Thanks, but I'll get it later. Right now, it might be best if you drop me off at my apartment in town."

"Okay," he said. "I'll need directions when we get closer to your place."

She nodded. "We still have a ways to go. But once we get off the main road, it's a quick shot up…"

Jonah had stopped listening. The black Jeep was back and close enough to reveal the silhouette of a tall, dark-haired driver hunched forward in the front seat. It had to be the same vehicle that followed them from the airport. And now—finally—he could read the numbers and letters on the front plate.

Minnesota TRX101. He'd run the sequence on his computer when he got home.

He tapped his brakes, anticipating that the Jeep would slow down accordingly. He half expected his move to cause it to drift back again, fading out of sight. Instead, the driver closed the gap even tighter, lingering mere inches from the bumper of his car.

What is this guy playing at? Putting aside the possibility that his own cover had been compromised, it seemed possible that whoever was following them was somehow involved in the shooting at the lake.

It was time to put some space between the two vehicles. Jonah pressed down hard on the accelerator, and the Subaru shot ahead. But the Jeep caught up in a matter of seconds, once again getting close and then closer, finally slamming into his bumper hard enough to push the Subaru into the opposite lane.

Beeeeeeep.

The driver of a delivery van, heading south in the opposite lane, frantically sounded his horn.

Beeeeeeep.

Jonah cranked the steering wheel to the right, just in time to avoid a head-on collision. But the car continued skidding, and the rocky lakeshore loomed only a few yards away.

It would be a quick drop into Superior's ice-cold waters.

"Hang on and pray," Jonah said. "It's going to be close."

Carmen braced for impact as the Subaru swerved toward the narrow shoulder on the right side of the road, pressing her right hand against the console and tightening her left around her trembling pup. Fear gripped her so tightly that she couldn't bear to look at Jonah. Instead, she focused on his hands, on his veins popping against his white skin as his fingers clutched the wheel. Time slowed down as the Subaru rotated in slow motion, skidding sideways toward the lake.

In the breath of one second that seemed like an eternity, the Subaru came to a shuddering stop, its front bumper jammed against a huge boulder, marking the drop into the lake.

Safe. Carmen blew out a long sigh. She turned to fix her gaze on Jonah, whose hands still retained their death grip on the wheel. "Wow. Where did you learn to drive like that?"

"From my dad. He was a firm believer in defensive driving. It sure paid off with that tailgater."

Tailgater? Maybe. Carmen wasn't sure she was buying Jonah's interpretation of their almost fatal collision. Road rage was certainly a common enough occurrence these days. But it was a lot more likely that this was no accident. The driver of the Jeep that had come up so fast behind them had to be somehow connected to what happened earlier at the lake.

"Should we check the damage to your car?" she asked, "So far, we're batting two for two today. First the plane, and now your Subaru."

"Later. Right now, I need to get us turned around before we get clipped by a passing motorist."

"My apartment building is at Fourth and Main. It's still about a mile and a half down the road." She sneaked a glance at Jonah as he backed away from the boulder and turned the car around. With his blond curls and strong jaw, he was undeniably handsome. *Trouble,* her mom used to say about men like him. *Avoid at all costs.* But the warning label didn't seem to fit Jonah. There was something solid and dependable there, something more than just good looks.

His blue eyes crinkled as he met and held her glance.

"Everything okay?" he asked, raising a

brow as he eased the Subaru back onto the highway.

"All good," she said as she tore her eyes away from his face and looked down at Bruno, still asleep on her lap. He really was a very sweet pup, especially now that he had passed the stage where shoes and chair cushions were viewed as convenient chew toys. Most people thought he looked like a Jack Russell terrier with his white fur and stubby tail. But the tan patches on his face and his large, floppy ears always made her think of a miniature beagle.

The first thing she'd do when she got back to her apartment would be to apply disinfectant to that nasty cut on his leg. Then, once she was sure he was okay, she'd borrow a cell to call her stepdad to ask if he could give her a ride to pick up her car.

She also needed to figure out the reason she had been attacked at the lake. It seemed obvious that someone was trying to stop her from digging into the cold case. But besides Chief Tuttle, only two other people knew of her plan to visit the cabin today—her stepfather and her stepbrother, Kirby. And it was hard to believe that either one of them would have passed on that information.

But a lot had changed since she left home over a decade ago.

For one, her stepfather had been in and out of jail on various charges. Clint always had a tendency to play fast and loose with the law. But although he often walked a thin line between respectable and shady, perpetually low on cash but ever optimistic in whatever latest scheme he was hawking, he really didn't have a violent bone in his body.

As for Kirby...well, she couldn't accept the fact that he would knowingly hurt her in any way. But he had been so volatile lately, constantly in trouble both at home and at school. And, according to Clint, Kirby had been hanging out with a gang from the trailer park where they lived, most with rap sheets several pages long. Could one of those so-called friends have been the man who had attacked her? It was possible. But what was the connection to the cold case?

"Is this where you live?" Jonah asked.

Carmen looked up. Jonah had pulled to a stop in front of a concrete-and-wood, fifties-style apartment building at the end of the block.

"This is it," she said, her glance taking in the mismatched off-white folding chairs and the pot of stringy, half-dead mums on the balcony of her second-floor unit.

Home sweet home. Two bedrooms and a small living room and kitchen. But you had to do what you had to do. As soon as Clint had called to ask for her help with Kirby, she knew she had no choice except to return to Foggy Falls.

Sliding out of the passenger seat, she moved around the car as Jonah stepped out onto the sidewalk in front of the building.

"Do you want me to come up with you to make sure everything's okay?"

She shook her head. Jonah was clearly a nice guy, but he had done too much to help her already. "You need to get home and taste whatever it is your daughter's been cooking. But don't forget that I want to pay for the damages to the plane."

"Like I said before, no worries," he responded.

She started to walk away and then paused and turned back to face him. "Hey, I wanted to ask you before, but then I forgot. Are you a Christian?"

He shrugged. "Born and raised. But at this point, somewhat fallen away... What gave me away?"

"It's just a little thing, but back there on the

highway, when that car almost drove us off the embankment and into the lake, you said, 'Hang on and pray.' And that made me wonder because I was already praying, so I was glad that you were, too."

The look he shot her was bemused—and amused. "Well, great. I'm just happy it all turned out okay."

So was she.

She waited until the blue Subaru pulled away from the curb before heading up the path to the front door. With the turn of her passkey, she was inside the deserted lobby of the building. Her usual routine was to take the stairwell, but today, she was so tired that she decided to take the elevator. As she pushed the call button, Bruno looked up at her, his gentle dark eyes extra bright and confused.

"It's okay, buddy," she assured him. "This way is quicker."

Bing!

The elevator floor still seemed to be moving when Carmen stepped inside. Her stomach roiled as they lurched upward on a five-second ride to the second floor. The door slid open to reveal a narrow corridor with beige walls and beige carpeting, infused with an aroma of stale food and cigarettes. There were only two units in this section of the building, with Carmen's the closest to the fire-escape door.

Her keys jangled as she fit the right one in the lock.

Click.

The mechanism caught. She turned the knob and stepped inside, feeling along the wall for the light switch.

Her fingers froze on the panel. Something wasn't right. Her ears registered the soft click of a door closing, and she had the sudden realization that she wasn't alone.

THREE

"Is this all you've got to eat…leftover lo mein and expired yogurt?"

"Kirby?" Carmen spun around to face her scowling stepbrother, who was leaning against the kitchen door. He was looking taller than usual thanks to the dark curls piled in a high peak above the shaved sides of his head.

"Kirby." She said his name again, softer this time as she recognized the vulnerability in his eyes. "Is everything okay?"

His lips cracked in the upward thrust of a dissatisfied smirk. "It's all good. I'm just tired of waiting for you to come home. When my dad gave me the key to your place, he said you'd be here two hours ago."

"Yeah, well. Something came up with work."

"Right. Work. Your favorite thing in the whole world. Maybe I should leave right now so I don't interrupt any important police business."

"What? No. I'm glad you're here. Just give me a second to…"

"What happened to your dog?" Kirby pointed at Bruno, who seemed intent on chewing a hole in his temporary bandage.

"He hurt his paw. Why don't you finish eating while I disinfect and rebandage his wound, and then I can help you with your homework."

"You wish. Sorry to tell you, but I'm not here for tutoring. I'm here because your dear old mom threw me out. No big surprise there. She's been waiting for an excuse to do that for months. I wanted to stay with one of my buddies, but for some reason, my dad said I needed to come over here. He claimed you'd be happy to have me." He blew a quick breath through his nose and shook his head. "Looks like he was wrong. You don't seem very excited about sharing your space with your favorite little brother."

Uh-oh. Was she that transparent? She needed to work on her poker face.

Because having Kirby show up on her doorstep was neither a disaster nor a surprise. Lynn Trainor had made no secret of the fact that she was getting fed up with her stepson's behavior and lack of respect. Then again, hadn't she made those exact same complaints about Carmen as a teen? Her mom had always been high-strung and volatile, easily triggered when her demands went unmet. Still, it couldn't be easy living in a double-wide trailer with a surly kid who knew all the tricks when it came to poking the bear and playing on his dad's sympathies.

But whatever the impetus for Kirby's arrival at her apartment, the opportunity to spend more time with her stepbrother was the reason she had returned to Foggy Falls. The timing wasn't the best, but what mattered was the chance to forge a bond with Kirby and prove to him that she cared.

"Kirby. I really am very glad to have you here. And I want to make sure you feel at home. Let me know if you need another blanket or pillow or any toothpaste or shampoo. I have extras of all that, and…"

Her stepbrother had stopped listening. Shoving the last tangle of noodles into his mouth, he stuffed the empty carton into the trash can and tossed his dirty fork in the sink. "I'd love to stick around and chitchat. But I gotta do some stuff. And just so you know, I'll have my headphones on, so I won't hear your dog if he starts barking because he needs to go out."

Carmen swallowed a sigh. It looked like this wasn't going to be the moment for kicking back on the sofa with her stepbrother and bonding over old memories. But on the off chance that Kirby changed his mind about talking, she'd back-burner her plan to retrieve her car.

"I leave for work around seven thirty tomorrow morning," she said as Kirby disappeared into the spare room. "Want me to wake you up before I go?"

"I'm not five years old anymore," Kirby's voice boomed through the closed door. "Don't worry about me."

She'd try not to. But it wasn't going to be easy.

After cleaning Bruno's wound with a cotton swab and Bactine, she settled down at her computer and caught up on her email, updating the case file to include the events of the day. The first thing she needed to do when she arrived at work tomorrow was to file a report on her missing weapon. It was a safe assumption that her assailant had pocketed it after she set it on the ground, but it was worth making sure.

Before she knew it, it was after six, and

Bruno was nudging her leg, expecting to be fed. An hour later, she was climbing into bed, exhausted, her own supper forgotten. At least the little pup had regained some of his usual spirit. He seemed to be smiling as he curled up in the nest of blankets at the foot of her bed.

"Goodnight, Bruno," she said with a smile. Mere moments after she hit the pillow, she was out like a light. If she dreamed about the pursuit at the lake or about the near collision on the highway, she didn't remember.

Her alarm sounded too early, propelling her out of bed, desperate to silence the high-pitched beeping before the blare woke up her new roommate. With one eye open, Bruno watched as she pulled on the navy uniform of the Foggy Falls Police Department, brushed her teeth and combed her hair. Tiptoeing into the kitchen, she filled Bruno's two-sided bowl with kibble and fresh water. After a short trip downstairs so the pup could do his business, she headed off on foot to the station.

Her apartment building's proximity to work was one of the major selling points when she signed the lease. And it was especially handy now that, even without a car or a phone, she could get to work and then use her lunch hour to head home to check on Bruno. And to make sure Kirby had left for school.

Please, God. Help that boy understand that getting a good education is worth the effort. It was embarrassing to remember what a terrible student she herself had been during her tenure at Foggy Falls High. Scratch that. Terrible was the wrong word. Distracted, maybe. Uninterested. Checked out. Whatever you'd call it, it had taken her way too long to get her priorities in order. All she had ever wanted to do was play hockey, but that part of her life had come to an abrupt end the horrible night she was attacked at the outdoor rink.

But, as one of her friends from LA used to say, God's light can't be shut out even in the darkest of storms. And it was in reaction to the events of her senior year that she had become the dedicated and focused officer she was today. Kirby had said that work was her favorite thing in the world, and he wasn't far off. Her job gave her purpose and satisfaction that she had never found in her personal relationships with family and friends. So why not put her time and attention into what she was good at?

By the time the station came into view, Carmen was more than ready to begin the day. All at once, she felt her worry and stress slip away. Here, like nowhere else, she was in control.

A bounce was in her step now. A strong wind whipped the station door closed behind her and pushed her toward to the reception desk.

"Is Chief Tuttle in yet?" she asked Lisa Carpenter, who raised a long, manicured finger and pointed toward the open door of the office, which afforded a view of the man himself, hunched over and staring at the screen of a computer in the middle of his desk.

"Chief?" She walked over and knocked softly on the door.

"Carmen." He straightened up and greeted her with a curt nod. Although not a tall man, he radiated confidence and self-assurance. "What can I do for you today? Rumor has it that your stepbrother moved into your apartment yesterday. Your mother must be dancing a jig."

Harsh, but true. Bill Tuttle had a pretty good handle on reading the citizenry.

"You probably knew about that before I did," Carmen said. "But I'm actually glad to have Kirby as a roommate. Maybe the extra time he and I will be spending together will make a difference. But that's not why I popped in to see you. I wanted to let you know that things didn't go exactly as planned yesterday when I was checking out the Larssen cabin."

Bill Tuttle pushed back in his chair. "Tell me about it."

Carmen settled into the closest of the two identical chairs in front of the chief's desk. It took her fifteen minutes to describe the events of the previous day, and then ten more to answer questions about her attacker.

"You need to look through the headshots we have on file. You know we don't have that fancy computer stuff like you had back in LA, but if you see someone who looks familiar, you let me know. I told you from the beginning I have your back on this one. I'll send someone out to Lake Isla to see if they can find your missing weapon. Until then, ask Lisa to issue you a backup. I have to admit I'm intrigued by the guy who rescued you in his Cessna. Not many people around these parts can afford their own private plane."

"I know. Right? He said he's a teacher at the high school with a kid. And a weekend pilot. But I don't think he's rich. The Cessna was a rental."

"Did you get a name?"

"Jonah. Jonah Drake. Seemed like a nice guy. I can hardly complain. He saved my life."

"Check him out anyway. And keep me updated, okay?" Bill Tuttle shifted his gaze back to his computer screen, signaling that the conversation was over and she was dismissed.

Carmen stepped out of the chief's office and headed for her desk. She did a quick search for *Jonah Drake Minnesota* in the police database and learned that Jonah was exactly the person he claimed to be—a Spanish teacher who had moved to Foggy Falls after a few years working at a magnet high school in the Twin Cities.

Next up was a transcript of an interview with the man who had found Sara's body floating in the lake. It was a tough read, even the fifth time around. Halfway through the pictures from the autopsy, Carmen needed a break.

Time for a cup of coffee.

And not the usual muddy sludge from the old percolator. She selected a pod from a basket on the counter and pressed it in the machine, taking a moment to inhale the bracing aroma of fresh-brewed joe.

Carmen stuck her head around the doorframe and called across the room to the receptionist, who was finally off the phone, "Hey, Lisa. Thanks for buying supplies for the Keurig."

"Thank *you*." Lisa's voice had a singsong quality that took some getting used to, but her smile was gracious as she pointed to the industrial-size box of coffee pods on top of the freezer. "Thirty bucks at Costco. And you put a twenty in the collection jar."

Cup of coffee in hand, Carmen returned to her desk and spent the next hour rereading old newspaper accounts of the Larssen case. The most interesting of the lot was an article that had appeared in the *Duluth News Tribune* about a twenty-two-year-old apprentice carpenter named Shane Rogan, who had been a close friend of Sara's. Initially, Rogan had looked good for the murder until one of his friends conveniently came forward to provide him with an alibi. The author of the article threw shade on the entire proceedings.

From across the room, the main line jangled. Lisa answered with a crisp "Foggy Falls Police Department. How can I direct your call?"

A minute passed before Lisa called out from across the room. "Carmen. You're going to want to take this. It's Donna from the high school."

Carmen headed toward the reception desk and reached for the phone in Lisa's hand. "This is Carmen," she said.

Donna didn't waste time with unnecessary chatter. She relayed the fact that Kirby had been suspended from school, disapproval dripping from every syllable. "We couldn't reach anyone on his contact list, and the assistant principal said I should tell you to get over here as soon as possible to pick him up."

"I'll be there as soon as I can." Carmen handed Lisa the receiver and headed back to her desk. She had almost made it to the door before remembering that her car was still at Lake Isla.

And the high school was four miles from the station.

She did a one-eighty and headed back to talk to the chief.

"Sorry to interrupt you, sir, but would you mind if I took a patrol car to the high school to get Kirby? Apparently, he stabbed a teacher with a pen."

Jonah wiggled his fingers back and forth, mimicking an exercise from back in the day when he was learning to play the piano. Anything to ease the pressure from the tightly wound compression bandage around his hand.

Slumped in a chair on the other side of the outer office was the person responsible for that throbbing pain—a kid named Kirby

Trainor, who had jammed his pen into Jonah's palm. It had been just the latest of this particular student's many infractions. Two weeks earlier, the teen had kicked out a classroom window and ended up with a week of detention. This time, the punishment would be a lot more severe.

With one foot jiggling nervously against the counter, Kirby kept his eyes fixed downward on his lap, picking at his ragged nails. The kid was high. High and unafraid. Jonah's gaze traveled to the poster over the door to the inner office: Foggy Falls High School Is a Drug-Free Zone.

Ha. Call him cynical, but he had a problem with any school making such a grandiose claim.

Kirby Trainor wasn't in any of his classes, though he had certainly seen him around the school. The kid kept to himself, so it was hard to get a good read on what had happened in the lunchroom. The more he thought about it, the less sense it made. Why would Kirby draw attention to himself like that when anyone with half a brain could tell he was under the influence? And what had the teen been thinking, throwing punches at a student twice his size?

Jonah wished he could ask the kid himself.

Who knew where a few questions might lead? It was unlikely he could persuade Kirby to give up his dealer, but it might be worth the try. However, Assistant Principal Max Mace had been crystal clear on the fact that, until Kirby's mom or dad arrived at the office, no one should discuss the incident.

And Jonah was proceeding by the book when it came to Mace. Intel suggested that someone highly placed at the school was dealing drugs to the students. And the assistant principal was a possible suspect.

Jonah glanced at the clock. The bell was going to ring in less than fifteen minutes. He ought to be prepping for his next class, but instead he had been roped into what was sure to be a lengthy discussion with the parents about Kirby's future. Whatever the reason, he was stuck here until…

There was a shuffle of footsteps in the hall. Maybe that was the mom or dad now. Jonah fixed his eyes on the door as—he pulled in a long breath—Carmen Hollis, looking very official in a crisp, blue uniform, entered the room.

He wasn't sorry to see her. In fact, he had been thinking about her just that morning before his first class, still surprised by the immediate attraction he had felt when they met. But her showing up here now was an odd development. Had the police been called to handle the incident?

Carmen seemed equally confused. "Hi," she said, her glance shifting back and forth between him and Kirby. A second passed, and the realization seemed to dawn. "Oh, right. Now I remember. You told me you were a teacher here at the school." Her glance took in the bandage on his hand. "And it looks like you were the one who was stabbed by Kirby."

"Well…" Jonah shrugged and attempted a smile. "Not exactly stabbed. More like punctured. The pen barely broke the skin. I should go on to live a long and happy life."

No one laughed at his joke.

Carmen turned to face Kirby. She looked like she had a lot to say. But before she could open her mouth, Kirby held up a hand to forestall the lecture. "Cool your jets, Carmen. It was an accident, okay? That's what Mr. Drake told Mace, so don't go thinking I attacked some teacher. Bobby punched me, and I hit him back. I just forgot the pen was in my hand." The kid's voice came out in a high squeak, causing Jonah to revise his initial assessment of the situation. The teen *was* scared. Not of the punishment, but of something else.

"Kirby's my brother," Carmen explained.

"I figured that," Jonah said as Assistant Principal Mace stepped out of the inner office.

"Everyone here? Good. Let's get started. I don't have all day."

Jonah bristled, put off by the man's imperious tone. Apparently, Carmen felt the same way. She noticeably recoiled as Mace stepped toward her, extending his hand.

"Great to see you, Carmen," he said. "I heard you were back in town, working for the police. I wish we had been able to meet under better circumstances. A ticker-tape parade seems a lot more in line to welcome our school VIP." Mace swiveled his head to bring Jonah in on the joke. "Carmen here was the best hockey player in our school's history. Most of the records she set in her first three years are still standing. If you don't believe me, you should check out the trophy case in the front hall. Of course, we don't need to talk about the rest of the story, do we now? But I've always wondered—do you still play?"

Carmen pretended she didn't hear the question. "Hello, Mr. Mace. Since we all know how busy you are, why don't we skip the catching up for now and get right down to discussing the reasons you called me here today?"

Kirby's snigger was perfectly timed as a tall, thin man with longish hair and camo jeans came storming through the door. He was around forty-five or fifty, with deep-set eyes, an angular face and an angry demeanor. The resemblance to the teen was unmistakable.

"What's going on?" He directed his questions to the assistant principal. "Why's Carmen here? I'm the first contact for issues with my son."

"We tried to reach you, Mr. Trainor." Mace's tone was thick as maple syrup. "But you didn't seem to be answering the phone. And Kirby told us he was currently living with Carmen."

"So? Why not leave me a message? I only found out about this when I phoned Carmen at the station and the receptionist told me she had gone to the school to pick up Kirby."

"Well, you're here now, so there shouldn't be an issue," Mace said,

"I do have an issue. But I don't have time to deal with any of this at the moment. I'm on the way to deliver a cord of wood to a customer. But, on the bright side, assuming you're kicking the kid out of school again, he can come along and help unload the truck. What do you say, Kirby? Grab your gear and let's hit the road."

Kirby stood up and moved to his father's side.

"Not so fast, Mr. Trainor," Mace said. "Before anyone goes anywhere, we need to discuss the details of your son's suspension."

But his intended audience was already out the door.

Mace slammed his fist down on the desk. "This is not acceptable," he said to no one in particular. Jonah looked over at Carmen, who also seemed poised for flight.

"I'll talk to Clint about this later tonight," she said, edging slowly toward the door. "He won't let Kirby off the hook on this. But since he's in charge at the moment, I'm going to get back to work." She raised a hand for a quick goodbye as she headed out the door.

Jonah made a show of checking his watch. "I need to take off as well. Fifth period starts in ten minutes." He flexed the fingers on his injured hand. "Like I said before, I don't want to make a big deal out of what happened in the lunchroom. The kid definitely deserves to be suspended, but I don't think he meant to jab me with his pen."

"Be that as it may," Mace said, "I'm still going to need a report."

"I'll have it on your desk by the end of the day." Jonah took off jogging down the hall. He needed to move fast if he wanted to catch up to Carmen.

"Carmen. Wait. Do you have a minute?" he said, falling in next to her as she reached the front door. "I was hoping we could talk. About what happened in the cafeteria and also about Kirby. I'm sure you know that he has been using. Pot, I'm guessing, though I can't say for sure it's not something more serious."

Carmen appeared taken aback by his candor. "I appreciate your interest, Jonah. But this is way too complicated to be solved by a short conversation." Her gaze dropped toward his bandaged hand. "I'm just sorry you got involved in my brother's issues."

Her brother's issues? What did that mean? Jonah didn't know anything about Kirby's background, but he knew quite a bit about Carmen's, thanks to the search of the BCA database he had done last night after Betty had gone to bed. Carmen's file made for interesting reading, but he couldn't help feeling like he was violating her privacy; though, as an investigator himself, he had a pretty good excuse. Because someone in the police department was likely involved with the drug smuggling, and though he was reasonably sure it wasn't Carmen, any and all information was key to a thorough investigation.

He had also spent some time tracking the license plate of the car that had been tailing them after they left the airport. It had been reported stolen two days earlier, proving to be yet another dead end. If only he knew a few details about Carmen's case. But it would be difficult to find out more information without blowing his cover.

As he stepped outside, Jonah's eyes were assaulted by the brilliant sunshine of a cloudless November day. The deep reds of a stand of maple trees along the main lot seemed to add a streak of fire to the afternoon sky. "It's so bright. I can hardly see in front of me. Where did you park?" he asked, reaching into his side pocket for his Ray-Bans.

Carmen pointed toward a row of vehicles along the rear of the lot. "I had to take a squad car since I still haven't managed to pick up my Honda from the lake. I parked in the back, next to the fence. I knew Kirby would hate it if I pulled in out front and everyone was left to wonder what was going on."

He checked his watch again. He still had

seven minutes to make it to his classroom. "I actually had a couple questions about yesterday. How about I walk you to your car and we can talk?"

"Okay. And I'd like to pin you down about the damage to the plane." Carmen kept moving forward as she opened her purse and pulled out a pen and a small pad of paper. "I updated the chief this morning about what happened. I still don't have a phone, but if you give me your contact info, I can make sure you get a check to cover the repairs."

"Most of the damage should be covered by insurance, so let's not get bogged down by that. What I actually wanted to talk to you about was…"

Bzzzzzzzz.

A mechanical whirring filled the air. Jonah looked up, scanning the sky for the source. A few seconds passed before he was able to locate what looked like a four-winged bug hovering about twenty-five feet in the air. He blew out a long sigh. The last thing he needed to deal with right now was a kid who ditched class to play with a drone in the parking lot. But how could he ignore such an obvious transgression? He took a few steps backward and scanned the vehicles along the back fence, looking for someone with a remote control who could be held accountable for the commotion.

Carmen reached out to open the patrol-car door as the sound got louder and louder and the drone began moving faster, speeding toward them. And it appeared that a cylindrical object was attached to the bottom of the drone, an object that looked suspiciously like…

"Carmen! A bomb! Look out!"

She took a step backward a half second before the flash of light and flare of heat engulfed the parking lot, tossing her body like a rag doll through the air.

FOUR

"Carmen!" Jonah repeated as the bomb blast reverberated through the air. The boom of the explosion had been so deafening that every other sound seemed muted in comparison.

He pushed himself up off the asphalt and ran toward the squad car. His mind registered the gaping hole in the vehicle where there was once a door and part of the roof, the debris still falling around him, grayish ash that seemed stuck in his throat along with the acrid stench of burning rubber. His blood thudded through his body as he forced his legs to move even faster.

"Carmen!" he shouted again.

And then it was as if someone had taken their finger off the mute button as a cacophony of noise broke through his senses. Screams echoed from all sides of the parking lot, the blaring bell of the school's fire alarm shrieked behind him, and the whir of sirens wailed in the distance.

He squatted down next to Carmen's limp body, his fingers instinctively pressing along her neck beneath her jaw to find the steady beat of a pulse. A sigh of relief escaped from his lips as his eyes roamed over the rest of her body, doing a quick assessment. Carmen was breathing, but the blast had clearly knocked her out. He glanced around the parking lot as the shriek of sirens pummeled his ears. What to do next? The EMTs would be on the scene in a matter of minutes. He rocked back on his heels, his fingers rhythmically tapping against his knees. Dare he try to move her?

"Ugh." A low moan emanated from the still form, followed by movement of hands flailing against the ground. "What? What happened?"

The truth seemed like the simplest option. "A drone dropped a bomb on your squad car. Don't try to move. Your injuries could be serious, and you most likely have a concussion."

His words didn't seem to register as Carmen pushed off the ground with her hands until she was sitting upright. "My car blew up?" She turned her gaze toward the wreckage and then back to him.

"You need to keep still. The police are on their way."

She blinked. Already the purplish tint of a bruise was beginning to form on her left cheek, and the sockets around both eyes were showing signs of swelling.

"We're at the high school." Carmen's voice didn't sound slurred or traumatized, or even confused. She seemed focused and intent.

He nodded. "That's right. Do you remember what happened?"

"I think so." She blew out a long breath. "You yelled for me to watch out. And then—" Her voice broke off, a sudden awareness seeming to register as her face tensed up and her eyes began to dart to the left and then right. "I have to make sure everyone is okay!"

Her body looked poised to spring into action, so he placed a restraining hand on her shoulder. "It doesn't look like anyone else was hurt. You were closest to the blast."

She shrugged off his hand and stood up. Her body swayed for a moment. Was she about to faint? His arms shot forward, ready to catch her, but she steadied her stance and began to make her way across the parking lot.

"The kids are going to be panicking. And what if there are more devices inside the building? We need to evacuate now." She began to weave unsteadily toward the entrance of the school.

A muscle clenched in Jonah's jaw. Now probably wasn't the best time to posit the theory that the bomb was clearly meant to kill Carmen, not random students at the school. But Carmen was not to be stopped as she made her way across the parking lot. Jonah scrambled to follow and in a few quick strides was at her side.

"You sit down on the steps and let me handle the evacuation. I can get started on a check-in system for the students exiting the school."

Carmen turned her gaze toward him, managing to convey a wealth of meaning in her raised eyebrows and the slight curl of her lips. "I don't think so, Jonah. No offense, but you'll just be in the way."

Right. He was supposed to be a civilian. But he couldn't sit still and allow Carmen to take charge. It was clear that the short trip across the parking lot had taken its toll on her. Her eyes were losing their sharpness and beginning to look glazed.

Frustration and something like grudging admiration simmered in the back of his mind as he recognized that even the shock of the explosion had not dimmed Carmen's determination.

"Let me see what I can do, and if I need

help, I'll come consult with you." He helped her sit down and then turned to assess the frenzy taking place all around them. Students were streaming out of the building and running in all directions, shouting into phones at their ears. Already a group of neighbors had entered the schoolyard and were moving forward to inspect the scene. A few teachers seemed to be trying to bring order to the chaos, but their efforts were ineffective at best. Where was the principal? Or the assistant principal, for that matter?

There! The silver head of Assistant Principal Mace appeared in the crowd. And he was carrying a megaphone! Jonah walked over to him, edging aside a few teenagers who were staring at the wreckage of the squad car. "Can you believe this?" Mace's face was drawn and distraught. "I assume that was Carmen Hollis's unit that just got blown up. Does anyone know if she got hurt?"

"She's a little shaken, but otherwise okay. I left her sitting on the steps by the main entrance."

Mace exhaled a shuddering sigh.

"Look, I'm going to need that bullhorn." Jonah reached over and took the megaphone from Mace's hand.

"Attention, please!" he shouted.

A few kids turned their heads, but other than that, his amplified voice was just another noise amid the tumult. His finger found the dial for the volume and turned it up. Once he flipped the switch from voice to siren, the wailing throb sliced through the commotion. He let it run for ten seconds, and then flipped the control back to voice.

"Attention!" he bellowed again. "Stop what you're doing and listen up." Most everyone froze and turned to look in his direction.

"We need order. Seniors. You need to congregate outside the library wing. Juniors and sophomores, remain on the front lawn, and freshmen, head down toward the field. Teachers, find the class you were teaching before the explosion. Take attendance. Anyone who is missing, notify me immediately. Now! Move!"

He turned his attention back toward the assistant principal, who was beginning to edge away toward the crowd. "The police will be here in a moment." He pointed across the lot toward the flashing red and blue lights racing down the road. "And they'll want to know who was present at the time of the explosion. To make sure everyone's accounted for, the teachers are going to need paper and pens."

"Right." Mace nodded.

"You and I need to go back inside and get the visitor log, first aid bags and anything else that might help sort out this mess."

He retraced his steps toward the front of the school with Mace behind him. But where was Carmen? Jonah scanned the crowd around the entryway. There she was, standing in the middle of a group of hysterical teens, trying to assist one of the teachers in rounding up her charges. As if sensing that he was looking at her, Carmen turned her head and caught his eye. He pointed toward the school, and she gave a nod of understanding.

The office doors were still open when he made his way inside. He grabbed the visitor log and the emergency binder with all the students' contact information and handed both items to the assistant principal.

"Take these outside and give them to the police."

Mace scuttled away, and Jonah entered the nurse's room that was attached to the office. He snatched up the first aid kit that was propped against the wall and then seized a ream of paper and a handful of pens.

By the time he made it back outside, the police were there, shepherding the faculty and students into a semblance of organization.

"Hey, mister." A young cop approached him from across the tarmac. "Are you okay?"

"Yeah. I'm fine."

"You know you've got a nasty scrape on your arm?"

Jonah looked down. Sure enough, blood was oozing through his shirt. His gaze traveled down to his hand, which was still bandaged from where Kirby had stabbed him with the pen. Two strange injuries in one day.

The surge of adrenaline that had been coursing through his body ever since he noticed the drone all of a sudden seemed to recoil from his limbs, leaving behind a sort of limp exhaustion. He looked again at his bleeding arm. It didn't hurt, but seeing the stark redness of the stain against his light blue shirt jolted his mind.

He had been just a few feet from a bomb explosion.

He could have died. Which would have left Betty without a parent.

And he had vowed to never let that happen again.

Carmen fidgeted as the bearded paramedic who had arrived with the ambulance shone a small light into her eyes, checking again to see if her pupils were dilated. "I see no signs of a serious concussion. But I'd recommend that you have a doctor check you out, maybe do a CT scan to make sure there's no swelling or bruising on your brain. After that, I'd suggest a few days of taking it easy. Considering what that bomb did to your squad car, it's amazing you're able to walk out of here without assistance."

"Thanks," Carmen said, stepping down from the ambulance. "I appreciate the advice."

It wasn't a lie. She did respect what the paramedic was saying. But she didn't have time for taking it easy.

Jonah caught up with her as she was making her way toward the orange police tape that had been strung across the lot. "How are you doing?" he wanted to know.

"I'm good," she said. "I just got checked out and was given the all clear."

"Really?" Jonah seemed incredulous.

"I can't stop to talk. I'm on my way back to the station."

"How are you getting there? I need to stick around to give a statement, but I'm sure I can slip out for a few minutes and take you where you need to go."

"Thanks, but I already set something up."

"Okay, then." Jonah seemed reluctant to end the conversation.

Carmen pointed toward Patti Phillips, a veteran officer on the force, who was waiting next to her vehicle. "There's my ride now. Thanks for checking in and making sure I was okay."

"Who is that guy?" Patti asked once Carmen was buckled in next to her in the cruiser.

"Jonah Drake. He teaches Spanish at the high school."

"Wow. They didn't have teachers like that when I was in school. He's really good looking. Not that you'd notice with everything else going on. I'm just glad you're okay. That was no firecracker attached to that drone. If you ask me, everything that happens these days is somehow connected to drugs," Patti said as she merged out of the lot onto the main road. "All that fentanyl that's being brought in from overseas is really bad stuff. I spent five hours last week at the emergency room, trying to get a lead on a dealer after two separate overdoses involving teens partying at the lake. Thankfully, both kids made it. But neither one was willing to give up his dealer. It's a travesty that the people profiting from the sale of this poison manage to keep their hands clean and remain above the fray."

All true. But if, as Patti had surmised, the bomb that blew up her squad car was connected to illegal drugs, why target the newest member of the Foggy Falls police force, who hadn't dealt with a single case involving narcotics?

"My office," Chief Tuttle said to Carmen moments after she walked into the station. He waited for Carmen to take a seat.

"You okay?" he said.

"I am. How about you?"

He raised an amused brow. "I'm not the one who almost got blown up. These next few days are going to be extra challenging. You want to hear the topper on all of this? So far, our guys inside the school have found fifteen bags of weed in a sweep of lockers outside of the classrooms and in the gym. So far, no fentanyl, but still." The chief settled back into his ergonomic seat and ran his fingers through the stubble of his beard. "And how is it that this Jonah Drake character has been on the scene for two attacks less than twenty-four hours apart? I know you checked him out on all the usual channels, but we somehow need to do a deep dive on this guy's background to see if there's something we're missing."

She saw his point. Jonah's presence at the

scene of both attacks was suspicious to say the least. As was the skill with which he had taken charge in the aftermath of the explosion. Still, he had come to her aid, saving her life twice—once by actually swooping in to rescue her in his plane. Carmen suppressed a prickling shiver brought on by the memory of yesterday's chase through the pines. If Jonah hadn't arrived when he did, she may not have lived to see another day.

"Go home, Carmen," the chief said. "There's nothing you can do here at the moment. I've sent a couple of officers out to see if they can locate your Sig as well as your phone, but I'm not expecting them to have much success. I assume the perp who came after you doubled back to the cabin to retrieve them, but we need to make sure. I'll let you know if they find anything."

"Great. I'll be here bright and early tomorrow," she said, pushing back her chair.

"Wait." Bill Tuttle reached into his desk drawer and pulled out a cell. "Take this. I asked Lisa to find a temporary phone that you could use until you get a chance to replace yours. It's old, so the battery won't hold a charge for all that long. But it's better than nothing."

"Thanks, Chief." Carmen pushed back

tears, determined not to let the chief see her cry. All day long, even as she opened her eyes after the explosion, she hadn't given in to the swirling emotions bombarding her brain. But now, overcome with the chief's thoughtfulness, she suddenly felt fragile for the first time that day. She was ready to go home.

It was soothing to walk along the tree-lined path to her apartment. And, as the perfect antidote to a difficult day, Bruno was waiting to greet her as she walked in the door.

"Who's a good dog?" she asked, scratching the spot between his ears where he loved to be petted. After a short walk outside, she returned to the apartment and pulled out her new phone.

She punched in the familiar ten numbers of the Trainor residence. She had been hoping to talk to her stepfather, but it was Lynn Trainor who answered on the second ring.

"Hi, Mom," Carmen said. "How are you?"

"How do you think I am? You could have called to tell me you were okay, but no. You're too busy to talk to your mother. And so is Kirby. I am sick and tired of dealing with your brother and the constant trouble he drops at our door. Of course, you don't know anything about that since you've spent the past twelve years hiding out in California."

Hiding out? Was that the spin to explain why her only child had quit the hockey team—quit school, in fact—and ended up moving to LA? *How about for once you tell the truth, Mom, and acknowledge the fact that you were incapable of understanding how awful it was when you refused to stand by me after I'd been raped?*

Of course, she didn't say any of that. That was a conversation for another day.

Or never.

"Is Clint around?" Carmen asked. "I'm wondering if he's planning to drop Kirby off here tonight."

"How do I know?" Lynn Trainor bit back in response. "That man doesn't tell me anything." The click of a lighter was followed by a whoosh of air as Lynn apparently took a drag on the ever-present cigarette dangling from her lips. "Except, now that I think about it, maybe I do recall Clint saying that after they delivered that wood, they'd be headed north for a week to some cabin belonging to one of his good-for-nothing friends."

The line went dead.

Which was her mother's way of indicating that she had nothing more to say.

Okay, then. Apparently, Kirby wouldn't be staying with her tonight, which was fine, although she wasn't quite sure how she felt about Clint's decision to take his son up north. Fishing in a lake and kicking back at a cabin didn't sound like much of a punishment after stabbing a teacher and getting suspended from school.

But what Clint decided to do with Kirby was not her problem. At least not today. She took a long, deep breath and punched in the digits of her next call.

"This is Mary at Foster Friends. How may I help you?"

"Hi. Yeah. This is Carmen Hollis. I've been fostering Bruno for two months now, and a few days ago, I got a text saying you found him a permanent home."

"Thanks for checking in, Carmen." There was a long pause as keys could be heard clicking on a computer. "I'm looking at the application right now, and I'm pleased to confirm that we have indeed found a lovely home for Bruno. A couple of newlyweds with a fenced-in yard who are looking to adopt a small, lively pup. Of course, they want to meet him. But Bruno appears to check all of their boxes."

Carmen swallowed hard, trying to dislodge the lump forming in her throat. This was the moment to ask if it would still be possible for her to keep Bruno. It was one of the things she wanted most in the world. So why was she hesitating? Lots of care providers go on to adopt the animal they had been fostering. Why not her?

She knew why. It was because she wasn't ready to make a permanent commitment. Bruno was the fifteenth dog she had fostered since starting in the program seven years earlier. And, like Bruno, several of them had lived with her for many months before a permanent situation had been found. And sure, she had gotten attached. How could she not, after spending almost a year looking into the eyes of Gridley, the earnest bulldog who loved to eat watermelon rinds and take long walks along the beach? Giving up Gridley had been hard, but so had parting ways with Louise, the mischievous Dalmatian, or Guy, the shy bull terrier whose eyes always seemed to brim with sympathy and compassion.

But she had understood the end game when she agreed to train and love those at-risk dogs and puppies, each time gritting her teeth and celebrating when the agency found them their forever home. After so many years volunteering with the program, first in California and now in Minnesota, the whole love-'em-and-leave-'em deal should have been getting easier, not harder. But that didn't appear to be the case.

This time felt different though. More gut-wrenching. Maybe she was just getting soft in her old age.

"Ms. Hollis?" said the woman from Foster Friends. "Are you still there?"

"Yeah. Sorry. I got distracted for a minute, but I'm here. Just let me know when the couple who want to adopt Bruno is looking to come by so I can make sure I'm home for their visit."

"Absolutely. I'll call them tomorrow. Thanks. Have a nice day."

The line went dead before Carmen could reply that, given the events of the past twenty-four hours, there would be very little that was nice in what remained of her day.

FIVE

*B*zzzzzzzz.

Carmen's eyes blinked open as she reached for the phone on top of her night table. "Hello?" she said, squinting at the screen.

"Carmen. It's Bill Tuttle."

Of course. No one else knew the number of her temporary phone. But why was the chief calling at—she glanced at the time—five thirty in the morning?

"Sorry to bother you," the chief said. "But an issue has come up concerning your step-brother."

"What now?" Even to her own ears, her voice sounded panicked. Her head still hurt, but when she gingerly touched her face, she could tell the swelling had already gone down.

"Now, don't get upset about this until all the facts are in and we know what we're deal-ing with. But late last night, officers searching the school found a remote-control device in Kirby's locker."

Her heart dipped in her chest. "For the drone?"

"For *a* drone. Not necessarily the one that carried the explosives. We'll know more once the technicians are able to reassemble the bomb and begin a trace on the components. But in the meantime, we'd like to talk to Kirby."

So would I. Despite the chief's not-so-subtle insinuations, she couldn't believe that her brother had been involved in the bombing. But it was the chief's job to ask questions to make sure. Carmen pursed her lips and blew out a long sigh. "My mom told me that Kirby and Clint were headed north to a friend's cabin. But I can check in with her once she finishes her shift at the diner and see if she can come up with an address."

"Tell her we'd appreciate her cooperation. Sorry again for the intrusion. I hope you can still get back to sleep."

Not likely. She threw off her covers and swung her feet over the side of her bed.

It sounded like the chief was already in his office. As soon as she fed and walked Bruno, she'd be there, too. Concussion or not, she wasn't going to ease up on her investigation.

* * *

The phones were already ringing when Carmen walked in the door.

Lisa Carpenter rolled her eyes in lieu of her usual greeting. "I just got in, but the chief's been here since four. I can tell already that it's going to be a crazy day."

Carmen headed straight for the open door of the chief's office. "Do you have a minute to spare?" she said.

Bill Tuttle looked up from the computer screen and nodded. He looked exhausted.

"Sorry to wake you this morning," he said. "After I hung up, I remembered that I hadn't even asked how you were feeling."

"Doing good," she said. "Glad to be part of the team."

Tuttle shook his head. "What I can't wrap my head around is the audacity of that sort of attack in the middle of the day. I know there's a rumor going around the station that the bombing is somehow drug related, but I'm not so sure. Until we get some answers, you need to be extra careful."

"You, too, Chief."

"Don't worry about me. By the way, I invited your friend Jonah Drake to stop by this morning for a second interview."

"Surely he isn't a suspect?"

"Not at the moment. He seemed pretty shaken when we took his statement yesterday at the scene. But if you're around, I'd like you to sit in on the interview."

"Of course," Carmen said. She turned and headed back to her desk.

When Jonah arrived an hour later, Chief Tuttle beckoned her to join them behind closed doors.

The chief waited until they were both seated. "Thanks for coming in again, Mr. Drake. This is a matter of the utmost seriousness, so I advise you to answer any and all questions in a truthful manner. Before we get started, I'd like to get Carmen up to speed on the statement you made about the explosion."

Jonah turned sideways in his chair. He seemed slightly tense, and her sympathies immediately kicked in at the tone of the interrogation. The chief was acting as if Jonah was somehow involved in the bombing, which simply couldn't be the case. At least not in her opinion.

"As I told you when we talked at the scene, Chief Tuttle, I didn't see the drone until it was already in the air. I thought it was some kid messing around with a toy. When the device dipped down toward the squad car, I noticed a flash of silver on the west side of the parking lot. I couldn't tell if it was the headlights of a car or a motorcycle."

"What happened after the explosion?" the chief inquired.

"At that point, I couldn't see anything through all the smoke and falling debris," Jonah said. "And my first thought was to check on Carmen."

"Thank you." Carmen hadn't said it before, but she was certain his warning had saved her life.

"I'll level with you, Mr. Drake," Bill Tuttle said, leaning forward with his elbows splayed out on his desk. "I find it extremely peculiar that you were present at not one, but two incidents involving Officer Hollis."

Jonah shrugged. "I get it. I'd probably think the same thing if the situation were reversed. But what can I say? I just read a story about two twins who had been separated at birth who met again when they both applied for a job at Disney World."

"Hmm." The chief appeared unimpressed with the unrelated coincidence. "And you spend your free time on the weekend flying along the shore of Lake Superior?"

Another shrug, this one longer and maybe a bit weary. "Some people golf or play tennis. I love to fly." Jonah pushed himself upright from his chair. "Sorry to keep this brief, but as I mentioned on the phone, I need to attend a meeting this morning at school. Classes have been cancelled, and there's a lot of concern from parents upset about the bombing and desperate to be assured that new safety guidelines are being put in place. Of course, there's also the issue of all the drugs that were found in the lockers. Maybe this will be the wake-up call the administration needs to take this problem beyond signs and silly slogans. Like the one in Mace's office. Drug-free zone indeed." He turned toward Carmen. "Speaking of Mace, I'd like to talk to you later if you have some time after work. Our assistant principal is pressuring me to press assault charges against Kirby. I told him no, but he doesn't seem inclined to let it go."

Carmen closed her eyes and pulled in another deep breath. She was beginning to understand how her mother felt about dealing with Kirby.

"Three thirty okay?" she asked, forcing a smile. "At the Coffee Depot on Pine Street?"

"Great. See you then."

Chief Tuttle waited until Jonah had exited the station before turning to Carmen. "What do you think?" he asked.

She shrugged. "Like I said before, I think he's a good guy."

"Maybe. Still. I'm glad you agreed to meet with him later. See if he lets down his guard and says something interesting."

What did the chief have in mind? Did he suspect that Jonah was keeping secrets? She didn't relish the idea of fishing for information, but even so, she found herself looking forward to meeting Jonah later that afternoon.

The Coffee Depot was a short walk, just a few blocks from the station, and Carmen arrived ten minutes early for the three-thirty meeting. She claimed a small booth inside the tiny restaurant, glad for the extra time to review her list of the things she still needed to do. Retrieve her car from Lake Isla. Buy a new phone since officers had been unable to find her old one at the cabin. Press her mom for information about the cabin where Kirby and Clint claimed to be staying. More immediate was her promise to the chief that she would find a way to break through Jonah's reserve to find out a little more about his background.

A chorus of brass bells clinked against the door, and Jonah walked inside. He had ditched his tie and khakis in favor of a sweatshirt and jeans, and he looked a lot more comfortable than she felt in her uniform. What had Patti Phillips said when she saw Jonah in the parking lot? "They didn't have teachers like that when I was in school."

Well, Patti had not been wrong, that was for sure.

"Hi." Jonah slid into the bench seat across from her in the booth. His eyes crinkled as he shot her a wide smile. "Thanks for meeting me. I'm going to see if I can order a cup of hot chocolate. What can I get you?"

"I'll have the same, thanks," she said, watching as he headed over to the counter and placed his order.

He returned to the booth, carrying a metal clip with the number seven, which he set in the middle of the table. "I got us a couple pieces of banana bread, too. Hey. I've been meaning to ask about your dog. Did you end up taking him to the vet?"

"No. I rebandaged the wound when I got home, and he seems to be making a good recovery."

"Glad to hear it. He seemed like a nice pup. He sure stayed calm, despite his injury. So…" he said, drumming his fingers on the table. "Let's talk about Mace and why he's so intent on me pressing charges against Kirby."

Carmen bit her lip and looked down at the table.

Jonah must have read the hesitation on her face because he shot her a rueful smile. "Sorry. I have a problem with subtlety. I didn't mean to jump right in with my questions."

"No. It's okay," she assured him. "I don't think Mr. Mace wanting you to bring charges has anything to do with a personal vendetta. He's probably just fed up with Kirby, and I can hardly blame him for that. Accident or not, stabbing a teacher with a pen was an impulsive and thoughtless move."

"I agree," Jonah said as the young girl who worked the counter set two steaming mugs and a plate of banana bread on the table. "But I would have expected Mace to let this go, especially with everything else going on. And maybe I shouldn't say this, but he seemed a bit thrown off his game when you walked into the office yesterday."

"I don't know why." She shrugged. "He was the one who told the school secretary to call me about Kirby being suspended. The fact is, Jonah, I've known Mr. Mace since I was in high school and he was the coach of the girls' hockey team. He wasn't happy when

I left town to live with my aunt in LA, but I'm sure he got over it. After all, it's just a game."

"He claimed you were the best player the school has ever seen."

"The whole team was good. We probably would have gone all the way to state if I hadn't quit. But I was working through a lot of issues at the time. Issues that seemed more important than scoring goals and winning the championship."

"I get it," Jonah said. His eyes brimmed with sympathy, almost as if he knew the part she had left out of the story, about how she had survived being beaten up, raped and left for dead. Maybe he did. He could have asked any of the old-timers at the high school about her past, and someone might have remembered the incident that drove her out of town.

Even now, if she closed her eyes and thought about it, she could still feel the sensation of being pulled down into the snow by a bearded man who had appeared out of nowhere at the rink. She had been so intent on lining up her shots that she never heard him approaching through the trees. He had a knife, and she knew immediately that he intended to use it. The searing pain of the blade being driven into her chest was as real today as it was twelve years ago. She might have died right then and there if it hadn't been for a passing taxi driver, dropping off a late-night fare, who had noticed her parka, bright green against the white snow.

But she didn't want to think about that now. The memory of what happened made her head spin and her stomach roil. She glanced down at the hot chocolate the waitress had set in front of her on the table and lifted the mug to her lips.

But she could feel the cup slipping out of her hand as a dark mist rose before her eyes. She flinched as the cup shattered in a half-dozen pieces as it hit the floor.

She stared down at the broken porcelain and then looked up at Jonah. Why did his face look so fuzzy?

That was the last thing she remembered noticing.

Jonah moved quickly to the other side of the table, just as Carmen's body slumped down into the booth.

Her eyes blinked open to stare at him. "Oh…hey. Sorry. I got a little dizzy there. I just need a moment, and I'll be okay."

"I'm not sure about that. My car's outside. What would you say to a ride to the hospital?"

She made a move to stand up but stopped

halfway. "No. I have to head home and take care of Bruno. And, really, I'm fine."

She didn't look fine. Only her vise-like grip on the edge of the table was keeping her body erect in the booth.

"How about this? I'll drive you to your apartment, and you can feed and walk your pup. After that, we can stop by my house and talk to my mother-in-law."

"Your mother-in-law?"

"She used to work as a nurse practitioner. She can make sure you aren't suffering the aftereffects of a concussion. It won't take long. Just a couple minutes for her to check things out and give you the okay." He stood up and held out his hand.

"Wait...no." Carmen shook her head. "I'm not sure this is a good idea."

"You can think about it on the walk to my car."

Forty-five minutes later, after a stop at Carmen's apartment to feed and walk Bruno, they pulled into the driveway of the three-story town house he had been renting since the beginning of the school year. The upside-down house, his daughter called it, with a living room and office on the first floor, the kitchen on the second and a trio of bedrooms on the top.

Carmen seemed a lot better now than she had in the coffee shop, but it was best not to take any chances. He led the way up the narrow steps of the porch and then inserted his key in the lock and pushed open the front door.

"Hello? Anybody home?" he called out, pretending not to notice the clattering sound of pots coming from the upstairs kitchen.

"Daddy!" Betty appeared like a cyclone, ready to knock down anything in her path. She stopped short when she saw Carmen. "Who are you?" she said. Her short hair looked especially disheveled, and there were globs of dough in it.

"My name is Carmen."

"Like Carmen Sandiego?"

"Exactly like that. I'm on a trip around the world, and people are trying to find me."

"Really?" Betty wrinkled her nose, baffled by the joke. "Well, my grandma's upstairs making dinner. She says that if I'm good next Sunday at church, she'll take me into Duluth to see the tall ships coming in under the bridge. Do you know about that?"

"Sweetie, Carmen knows all about Duluth. She grew up around here and probably went to see the ships all the time. But maybe you can do something to help me right now. Can you go ask Grandma to come down here for a minute? "

"I'll tell her Carmen Sandiego is here," Betty said as she disappeared up the stairs.

"Do you want to sit down?" Jonah asked, pointing to the sofa in the living room off the central foyer. The wary look on Carmen's face as she perched on the couch made him suspect that she was regretting the visit.

Footsteps sounded on the stairs, and a moment later, his mother-in-law appeared in the doorway. "Hello," she said, extending her hand to Carmen. "I'm Elizabeth Jensen, part-time cook and full-time grandma."

"And fully licensed nurse practitioner," Jonah added. "Liz, Carmen's the police officer I told you about who was injured in the explosion at the school."

"Oh, my dear, I am sorry," Elizabeth said. "Jonah said you suffered a nasty bump on your head."

"Grandma, something's burning in the oven!" Betty called from upstairs.

"Sorry." Carmen pushed herself up and took a step toward the front door. "I really didn't mean to intrude. Jonah was worried when I got a bit woozy at the coffee shop, but I feel so much better now. And I can see that you're in the middle of making dinner."

"Nonsense," Elizabeth said. "Jonah will take you home whenever you're ready. But before you go running off, I'd love to chat and maybe have a cup of tea, if Jonah doesn't mind making it, and turning off the stove while he's upstairs."

"Tea sounds nice," Carmen agreed with a half-hearted smile.

Jonah shot Elizabeth a grateful look. His mother-in-law truly was a wonder at always knowing the exact right thing to say. He couldn't imagine what his life would have been like if she hadn't moved in to help him when Julie died.

As he headed up the stairs to the kitchen, he could hear Liz asking for details about the bomb blast at the high school. No doubt about it, she would make sure Carmen wasn't experiencing serious side effects from a concussion. Jonah took his time preparing a tea tray, and when he returned with it, Carmen and Elizabeth were still discussing her symptoms.

"Your eyes look clear. No headache, confusion, memory loss or vomiting. The dizziness you experienced earlier may just be a sign of the stress and fatigue. But, of course, you still need to take it easy and not push yourself too hard."

"Thank you, Elizabeth," Carmen said.

"It's reassuring to be checked out by a professional. But I've taken you away from your duties for too long. Jonah, if you're still offering, I'll take a ride home."

"Here's an idea," Elizabeth said. "Why don't you join us for dinner?"

It was hard to tell what convinced Carmen to accept his mother-in-law's spontaneous invitation. Maybe she was hungry, or maybe she was just being polite. In any case, he was glad when she decided to stay.

A half hour later, Elizabeth cleared the table and shooed them downstairs into the living room.

"I like your uniform," Betty said. "Do you like it, too?"

Carmen nodded. "I do. When I put it on, I always think about what it means to protect and serve as a member of the force."

The girl nodded. "Did you always want to join the police?"

"No." Carmen laughed. "When I was your age, all I wanted to do was play hockey."

"Why?" Betty asked.

"I guess because I was good at it."

"Dad promised to teach me to skate. But I don't think he really knows how. We went to a rink once when we lived in Minneapolis, and he fell down. A lot."

Busted. "Hey. That's a slight exaggeration. But remember that I was stuck using an old pair of skates. Next time…"

"I think Carmen should teach me," Betty said.

"Um. I could do that," Carmen said. "But right now, it's still too warm for the outside rinks."

"Grandma says it's going to get colder in a couple of days." Betty's wide grin stretched across her face. "So you can teach me then. Hey, Carmen. Do you want to listen to my dad read *My Father's Dragon*?"

Jonah cleared his throat. "Betty? Since we have a guest, how about we skip tonight and read two chapters tomorrow?"

Betty's smile collapsed into a frown. "But it's really getting exciting."

"No worries," Carmen said. "I'm more than happy to sit here and listen."

Elizabeth stuck her head through the living room door. "If you three don't mind, I'm going to make a couple of phone calls that I've put off all day."

"Thanks for the advice and the wonderful dinner," Carmen called after her.

"It was a pleasure," Elizabeth said. "Help yourself to another cookie from the tray. And if you need the powder room, it's the second door to the left at the end of the hall."

Jonah opened to chapter three and began to read, but Betty's eyes were closed before he finished the second page. "Time to say good-night, sleepyhead," he said as he lifted her up into his arms and carried her to her room.

He was probably upstairs less than five minutes, but when he returned to the main floor, Carmen was nowhere to be seen. The powder-room door was open, but no one was inside. Had she gotten tired of waiting and decided to walk home?

From the office at the end of the hall came the scrape of a chair against the wood floor.

He headed down the corridor. The door swung open with an easy push. And there was Carmen, standing next to his desk, peering down at a map of Lake Superior.

A map he had marked with red circles, with the designation "Possible Fentanyl Drop Sites" written in bold letters across the top of the page.

SIX

Carmen lifted her gaze from the map on the desk.

"Possible fentanyl drop sites, huh? I guess I should have known you were law enforcement." She took a step backward and put her hands on her hips. "Which is it? FBI? DEA?"

Jonah pulled in a deep breath. Carmen's attempt at bravado might not have bothered him under different circumstances. But right now, he was far from amused. He was angry. And resentful. He had invited her into his home, and this was how she repaid him—by deliberately prying into his personal affairs.

But if he were being honest, he actually blamed himself more. How could he have been so careless as to leave the map out in plain view? He was usually so meticulous about securing classified information in his desk drawer. And even though he had forgotten his usual protocol last night, it normally wouldn't have mattered. His home had always been his sanctuary, and he rarely—if ever—invited others in.

Until now. Until Carmen invaded his personal space and erased months of work cultivating his cover as a teacher at Foggy Falls High. And all of that happened because he had put aside his usual caution in favor of his concern for her. How had he allowed himself to forget that she was a cop with the Foggy Falls Police Department, and as such, part of an organization full of leaks and possible ties to actual corruption? He needed to be more vigilant. He couldn't make a mistake like that again.

His displeasure must have been visible in his countenance because Carmen was quick to defend her actions and even offer an apology of sorts.

"I'm sorry, Jonah. I didn't intend to pry. I took a wrong turn in the hall. Your office door was open, and, well…what kind of an investigator would I be if I didn't notice the map of the lake in the middle of the desk? That's what you were doing in the Cessna, right? Monitoring the sites where they're bringing in the drugs from Lake Superior?"

Was she really expecting an answer? Did she think he was likely to break down and explain the scope of his investigation? That, after three months of maintaining his cover, he would fold and tell her everything?

Not likely.

And though he didn't suspect that Carmen was actually involved in any police corruption—the leaks extended back at least three years, maybe even a decade or more—he had no intention of letting down his guard. Any information, carelessly repeated, could put his investigation at risk.

Time to change the subject and go on the offensive.

"Let's talk about you instead," he said. "Because I'm not the only one keeping secrets. Want to explain what you were doing when I picked you up at the lake?"

Carmen tilted her head to the side. "I already told you. I was working a case."

"But why the secrecy?"

"It's complicated."

"Complicated because…" he prompted.

"It's actually a cold case that wasn't handled properly. This time around, we want to do things by the book."

"You say 'we.' I assume that means you and Chief Tuttle?"

Carmen nodded but didn't seem inclined to offer any more details.

Well, he could wait her out. Silence was an effective interrogation technique, and he wasn't in any hurry. He drummed his fingers against the desk and maintained eye contact with Carmen. After about half a minute, she ducked her head and pulled in a sigh.

"Look, Jonah. I need you to understand that my cold case is replete with its own unique issues. It's not exactly top secret, but it isn't an open investigation either. The officer who was originally in charge let too many things fall by the wayside. He homed in on a suspect early on and failed to pursue other, more viable leads. When Bill Tuttle got promoted last year, he saw the problems but decided that he didn't want to come in firing on all cylinders." Carmen's voice trailed off, as if she realized she had just given up more information than she intended. Her gaze caught his again, and her tone became tinged with a defensive edge. "But why do you want to know about this? What does it have to do with drug smuggling?"

He shrugged. "Nothing. But I'm a cop, too. And the circumstances are intriguing."

"Intriguing?" She paused before answering her own question. "Yeah. I guess I can see that. But is that the only reason?"

Good question. He didn't like to lie, but he

did wonder: Was he being honest in suggesting that his interest in the case was purely academic? Now that he knew Carmen was digging into an old murder, it seemed unlikely that there was any connection to his own investigation into the drugs. But after witnessing several attempts on Carmen's life, he could feel an unwelcome protectiveness begin to surge in his veins.

He tamped down his emotions and continued his inquiry.

"That's why you took the job in Foggy Falls? To work the case?"

"It was one of the reasons. Not the only one. As I told you before, I came back mainly because of Kirby." She smiled as she pointed to the wooden chair next to the desk. "Do you mind if I sit down?"

Carmen's straightforward demeanor tugged at his heartstrings. He wasn't used to such candor, but he was determined to not allow emotions to cloud his judgment. "Go right ahead." He stepped to the side and took the seat opposite her. "So, you went to Lake Isla to get fresh eyes on the crime scene?"

"That's right. That was where you spotted me running on the trail."

He sensed her frustration and softened his tone. "You didn't recognize your assailant?"

"I did not." She paused and met his eye. "But c'mon, Jonah. Fair is fair. I've answered your questions. How about you answer mine?"

He pulled in a sigh. Carmen's point was valid, but her case and his were not comparable. "At this point, you already know more than you should. There are good reasons why I'm undercover, Carmen. And I need you to respect that and not share any of the information you saw here tonight."

"But…"

"That's all I can tell you at the moment. But I do have one final concern. What you described about the scene at the lake sounds like an ambush. I just wonder who else knew about your plans last Sunday."

A shadow crossed her eyes. "Just the chief."

"Anyone else?"

She shook her head no.

Jonah took a deep breath. He had a fairly good sense of when someone wasn't telling the truth. And it was clear that Carmen was hiding something or protecting someone. But why?

A floorboard creaked from the other end of the hall. A moment later, his mother-in-law, clad in a light blue, downy robe, walked into the office. "Sorry to interrupt, but I wanted to let you know that I'm upstairs reading in case you need to leave to drive Carmen home."

"Thanks, Liz. We'll be heading out in just a few minutes."

"Sounds good. Take care, Carmen. I hope I'll see you again." Elizabeth smiled and then turned and headed up the stairs.

Five minutes later, Jonah was putting the car into reverse and heading down the driveway. An uneasy silence had settled between him and Carmen. Not that he could blame her. She had been collegial and shared information about her cold case, while he had essentially stonewalled all of her attempts to glean details about his assignment. Still, he wished there was a way to recapture some of the camaraderie that had been building between them prior to her discovery of the fentanyl drop sites.

Apparently, Carmen must have sensed the same disquiet because after a few minutes she broke the silence. "Elizabeth is lovely," she said at last. "I'm glad you insisted I get her input on my concussion. I detected a slight accent. Is she originally from the Twin Cities?"

He welcomed the change of topic. "No. She's from St. Louis. Her husband died ten years ago. My wife was her only child."

"I can't even begin to imagine how difficult it must have been to lose your wife."

His usual response to these kinds of comments was to shut down the conversation before it got too personal. But Carmen had been so forthcoming and straightforward that he felt like he owed her some answers. If he couldn't talk about the fentanyl investigation, at the very least he could chat about his personal life on the five-minute drive to see Carmen home. "Yeah. It was hard. A couple of times, I thought we weren't going to make it. Liz deserves all the credit in getting us through. Listen, Carmen. I hope we can put what happened tonight behind us and maybe meet on neutral turf sometime this week to discuss what's going on between your brother and Mr. Mace. You name the time and place, and I'll make it work."

Another several seconds of silence filled the car. He glanced at Carmen. Her face didn't look tense, but there was a speculative look in her eyes. "How about Friday night?" she finally replied. "I teach an hour-long self-defense class at the gym that begins at five. Any time after that would be great if you wanted to try the Coffee Depot again."

Carmen placed her hand behind her neck and rolled her shoulders up and down. Even though Elizabeth had given her a clean bill of health after she had fainted, she hadn't been feeling like herself the last few days. Stress had been building in her upper back, and, despite the ibuprofen she had been taking for the pain, a tightness was stiffening down her spine. Everyone had been advising her to take it easy after the explosion, but that wasn't the problem. It wasn't as if she didn't know what it felt like to fall and hit her head. She'd spent most of her childhood playing pond hockey with the older boys in the neighborhood. A solid check with no boards would usually send her sprawling on the ice, her legs skidding out from under her.

No, it wasn't the aftereffects of the bomb that were causing her worry. It was the realization that she might never be able to solve Sara's case. Patience had never been her strong suit, but the drive to find answers had always served as a great motivator. But even her usual tenacity was failing her now.

On the positive side was the news that Kirby was in the clear regarding the remote control involved in the bombing. The device found in his locker had turned out to be wholly defective, possibly—as the chief suggested—brought to school so her brother could work on a repair.

And, while the puzzle surrounding Jonah was partially solved, the discovery that he was in law enforcement raised more questions. What agency was he with? And why was he so guarded about his information? It had been an honest mistake when she opened the door of Jonah's office, but—she'd be the first to admit it—the rest of what had happened had been just plain old snooping. Obviously, Jonah had been angry at her—rightfully so—and, by way of an apology, she had allowed him to turn the conversation to a discussion of her case. But among those in law enforcement, sharing information was a two-way street, and even though he needed to maintain his cover as a teacher at the school, he also needed to recognize that as a local cop, she had as big a stake in what was going on with drugs in the area as he did.

If only she could discuss it with Chief Tuttle. But that was out of the question. She had given Jonah her word that she'd do her part in making sure he retained his cover, but the deception didn't sit well with her, particularly when it came to keeping secrets from the chief.

Carmen let out a long sigh and pinched the bridge of her nose. This kind of thinking wasn't getting her anywhere. She needed to shake off her worries and focus on the positive.

Lord, please give me wisdom. Please guide my thoughts and help me find the truth.

As always, the simple act of turning to Jesus brought a calmness to her churning mind.

Beep. Beep. Beep. The alarm on her phone chimed a reminder. Well, that settled it. Time to pack up and call it a day. At least at the precinct. She had thirty minutes to go home, feed Bruno and take him out for a short walk before heading to the gym for the weekly self-defense course she taught every Friday evening. And after that, she'd meet Jonah at the Coffee Depot.

An hour and twenty minutes later, she truly felt revived. The physical exertion of demonstrating how to ward off an attacker had loosened her limbs. Blood thrummed through her body, and a vitality she hadn't felt since first regaining consciousness after the explosion sharpened her senses. She couldn't help but smile with the contentment and satisfaction that came whenever she had the opportunity to teach the life-saving skills of self-defense. Skills she could have used had she known how twelve years ago.

She pulled an old LAPD sweatshirt from her duffle and dragged it over her head, then slung the bag on her arm and headed for the exit. The gym was an old converted warehouse. Nothing like the fancy spa-like fitness centers that populated southern California. But the Spartan facilities added to its authenticity and didn't seem to deter the locals from turning out for her class. Today she'd had nine students, five women from the local community college, an elderly couple who were worried about the rise in geriatric assaults, a lawyer and a lanky teenager whose sullen demeanor was in stark contrast to her enthusiasm for throwing the larger participants to the ground.

As she pushed open the door of the gym, a brisk, northeast wind sent shivers up and down her arms. It was supposed to be a cold winter this year with the snow already forecast for next week. She shivered as she flexed her fingers inside her gloves. It really was cold. She reached behind her to pull up the hood of her sweatshirt, when all the hairs on her neck suddenly stood on end. Her ears picked up the soft tread of footsteps too close behind her. She reached into her bag for the can of mace in her purse.

Too late. Her assailant pinned her arm behind her back and then clapped a mittened hand over her mouth, pinching her nose until she couldn't breathe.

For the beat of half a second, she allowed panic to rise in her chest, slowing her reactions and tempering her instincts. Her body, which had felt so vibrantly alert only minutes ago, was suddenly leaden with the fatigue of fear. Her mind slipped back to twelve years ago…no, no. She couldn't allow herself to go there. She couldn't allow herself to feel weak and vulnerable.

"Can't you take a hint?" a voice growled near her ear.

Hearing the high male voice was like responding to the buzzer at the start of a hockey game. Instinct took over. Along with the desire to win.

She wasn't that terrified teenager anymore. She was a cop. She taught self-defense. There was no way she was going to be taken out in the parking lot of her own local gym.

Take a hint? Not so much.

Ignoring the ache in her lungs from oxygen deprivation, she brought down the full force of her weight on the foot of her attacker. There was a stifled yelp and a muffled oath, and his grip slackened for just a moment. But a moment was all she needed. She pulled her left arm from between them and then swung backward with her elbow as hard as she could into the gut of the man behind her.

It was self-defense 101, but would it be enough?

No, the hand against her mouth only pressed that much harder. But now she had one free arm, which was sufficient to change the balance of the attack. Her fingers fumbled in her pocket for her keys. Then she heaved her body forward while twisting so she now faced her assailant.

Her mind registered the details. He was wearing a ski mask, so his face was covered, but he couldn't disguise the fact that he was over six feet tall. Average weight. Black windbreaker. And that voice—it was almost familiar but not quite, a blast from something in her long-forgotten past. Even as she cataloged this information, she swung her arm around, thrusting forward the point of the largest of her keys.

"Yowl!" The high-pitched cry didn't sound human as the man behind her screamed in pain, clutching his eye and staggering backward.

She didn't hesitate. She rushed forward, eager to seize upon her advantage. But the agony of his injury, rather than weakening her opponent, seemed to have enraged him. He caught her mid lunge, pinned her arms to the side and then threw her down on the ground.

Carmen felt a thud as her back hit the hard

cement and the breath was knocked out of her. Then his shadow loomed over.

She let out an earsplitting scream.

The man paused for a minute and then took off running. In one fluid motion, she rolled onto her side and pushed herself up. She filled her lungs with a big gulp of air and then took off in pursuit.

But between the headache that had been plaguing her all day and the adrenaline spike from the attack, she could feel the energy being sapped from her limbs. Her run slowed to a jog as she turned at the corner, scanning the darkness for her assailant.

SEVEN

Jonah turned his head as the streetlight caught the shadow of a woman as she ran past the window of the Coffee Depot.

Carmen. He'd recognize that long, dark hair anywhere.

He took off out the door. But by the time he caught up with her, she had almost reached the end of the block.

"Carmen. What's going on?"

"Some guy tried to choke me," she said, bending over to catch her breath. She straightened up and pointed toward the end of the street. "He headed north on Seventh. Where's your car? Maybe we can catch him before he gets to the main road."

Unlikely. Especially since his Subaru was parked two blocks from where they were standing. He pulled his cell from the pocket of his jeans and punched 911 on the screen.

"My name is Jonah Drake, and I'm calling

to report an assault on an officer at Seventh and VanNyes. Right…right… I'll stay with her while we wait." He slipped the phone back into his pocket and turned to face Carmen.

"They'll be here in a few minutes." He looked at Carmen and did a quick assessment. She seemed okay. No evident cuts or bruises. But her eyes brimmed with fiery determination.

"Do you want to sit down?" he asked, pointing to a small bench a few yards away.

"No. I'm fine. Really. Just embarrassed to realize that I got attacked on my way out of my class on self-defense."

"Was it the same person who was chasing you at the lake?"

She shook her head. "No. This guy was older and bigger. A lot bigger. At least six two and over two hundred pounds. I didn't get a very good look at him. He was wearing a ski mask and a black jacket. I can't believe I let him get away."

"Sounds like he had the advantage of height and weight. Not to mention the element of surprise."

"I'm a cop, Jonah. I'm not supposed to be caught unaware like that."

With a single blast of a siren, a black-and-white squad car pulled up to the curb. As both doors swung open, Carmen stepped forward to greet the two officers, who closed the circle around her to conduct the interview.

Jonah leaned against a stone wall along the side of the road and watched the proceedings. Carmen seemed to be doing all the talking as the younger of the two officers took notes on what she had to say. Apparently it wasn't much, because ten minutes later the two men climbed back into their vehicle and drove away.

Carmen walked over to the spot where Jonah was standing.

"They're going to set up a roadblock and cordon off the main road leading to the lake," she explained. "Though it's probably too late to do much good."

"I think we should get out of here as well. Maybe head back to my house to talk things through." Jonah's lips formed just the smallest smirk as he smiled and shook his head. "Don't worry. All confidential documents have been dutifully stowed away. And Betty and Liz are off at one of those paint-your-plate places tonight. But I can do my best to rustle up something for dinner."

Ten minutes later, Jonah stepped ahead of Carmen to turn on the kitchen light.

He waited until she sat down before he

began assembling the ingredients for dinner. "Fresh rolls, ham, provolone, turkey, Muenster, pickles, salami. It's almost like a deli with all of these choices. What sounds good to you?"

"Maybe just a glass of water to start."

"I can do better than that." He filled a glass from the tap and set it down in front of her. "I'm going to make you a sandwich. Turkey and cheese, okay?"

"That sounds delicious." Carmen looked down at the table and started to laugh. "You know what's crazy? I was going to mention it when I was here for dinner, but I bought the exact same dining room set as this one here when I moved to town. Our tastes must be similar, though I must say, it looks a lot better in your place."

"I can't take any credit for the decor. Liz picked most of our furniture out. Reluctantly, I have to say. She can't seem to get over the fact that we left most of our stuff behind when we relocated to Foggy Falls."

"Why did you?"

"Mayo?" he asked, pointing to the jar inside the refrigerator.

"No, thanks," she said. "Why did you?"

"Sorry. What?"

"Why did you leave so much behind? Why such a rush to move up here from the Cities?"

"It wasn't, really. Mustard?"

"Plain is fine. But what's with the stone-walling? Are you really not planning to share even the smallest bit of information that relates to the case? I understand there are limits to what you can tell me. But I may be able to help if you'd open up just a little bit. We're all on the same team here. You know about Kirby. How many other kids like him are getting pulled in by the easy availability of drugs at the high school?"

Too many. Even though it was eighteen years in the past, the overdose death of his older brother was something he would never forget. Over time, he had come to understand that the anger he felt toward Jerrod was unreasonable and unfair. His brother had been an addict in a time and a place where such things weren't always dealt with directly, at least not in their little farm town in western Iowa. Neither of his parents had a clue that Jerrod had been stealing money from friends and neighbors to support his habit. And none of their extended family or friends recognized the seriousness of the problem until his brother was gone.

Except Jonah. He had warned his parents that his brother was taking drugs, begged them to get Jerrod the help he so desperately needed. But no. His mom and dad were way too focused on their upcoming retirement and the plan that Jerrod would take over running the farm. And why should he continue to tell them what they didn't want to hear? He had his own big plans in place to become a cadet at the Air Force Academy. But then, two months shy of Jonah's eighteenth birthday, Jerrod died. Suddenly, everything changed. Jonah needed to be the one to stay home to help run the farm.

"Jonah?" Carmen's soft voice brought him back to the present. "I'm starting to wonder if you don't want to confide in me because you suspect that someone at the station is involved in some way."

He knew Carmen was a good detective from reading her file. But while he respected her credentials, there was a limit to what he was willing to say.

"My job is very specific and limited to surveillance. I don't want to lie to you, Carmen. But this whole thing is a lot bigger than my small part in the investigation."

Carmen picked up her sandwich and took a bite, chewed then wiped her mouth carefully on the napkin he provided. "This is good," she said with a smile.

"The key is the fresh bread from Margo's Bakery."

For a couple minutes, they ate in companionable silence. Jonah let his shoulders unclench as he imagined that they had tacitly agreed to let the subject drop, to enjoy a moment together as friends. Is that what they were becoming as they navigated the paths of their parallel investigations? It seemed like it, but what did that mean?

Since Julie's death, he hadn't done much in the way of maintaining old friendships, choosing instead to focus on work and Betty. Any attempts at social interactions had felt awkward and clumsy, with his friends avoiding any mention of Julie and skirting all references to his pre-widower life. But somehow, with Carmen, there was an ease to their conversation, a comfort level he hadn't felt in five years.

And maybe even something more.

Carmen took a sip of water and then turned to face him. "So, I'm thinking that you work for the DEA."

He let out a long sigh. Apparently, she was not going to let up on this until he provided some basic information. And it seemed she had already guessed most of his secrets on her own.

"BCA," he said, using the shorthand for the Minnesota Bureau of Criminal Apprehension.

"Does this have something to do with Mr. Mace?" she wanted to know.

"I don't know, Carmen. But I sure would like to talk to your brother. I have a feeling he may have information that could be incredibly useful in building our case."

A door slammed in the downstairs foyer, followed by the clomp of footsteps on the stairs.

"Sad news!" Betty said, rushing into the kitchen, her jacket hanging loose from one of her shoulders and two wispy pigtails sprouting from the top of her head. "We had to leave our plates behind. They still need to get baked. In an oven. But don't worry," she said as Elizabeth appeared behind her, shaking her head. "We can pick them up at the store tomorrow. You're going to love mine. It's pink and purple with a rainbow and a heart." She turned her head, suddenly aware that her dad had company. "Oh, hi, Carmen. Did you come by to take me skating? I don't think I can go tonight since Grandma says it's already past my bedtime and tomorrow's going to be a busy day."

Carmen smiled. It really was true that kids

didn't forget. But she had started to regret her offer to teach the little girl to skate. It had been twelve years since she had strapped on her battered brown hockey skates, twelve years since she stepped into a rink.

"Carmen's pretty busy, hon," Jonah interjected. "The skating lesson may not happen for some time."

"I can't wait." Betty began racing in circles across the floor. "Look at me, Carmen. I'm sliding across the ice."

"Very impressive," Carmen said. She was finding it impossible not to be charmed by Betty. Hadn't she been close to that same age when she first learned to skate? She had been four years old when her father left, and she and her mom had moved out of the house and into the trailer. Even then, she knew that skating lessons were her mom's way of making up for all the changes that had disrupted her life.

Jonah stood up. "Liz, if you don't mind holding down the fort, I'll give Carmen a ride home and be back in a jiffy."

"No problem," Elizabeth agreed.

It was a short drive to Carmen's apartment. Jonah pulled up in front, killed the motor and then turned to face Carmen.

"I'm sorry that Betty put you on the spot tonight. Since your last visit, all she's talked about is learning to skate. She's been like that since she was little. Once she gets an idea in her head, she won't let go of it. I don't think she really understands that it's not going to be as easy as the Olympians she's seen on TV. And Liz and I tend to be pushovers in these kinds of situations. I think we're both trying to overcompensate for the fact that she doesn't have a mother."

Carmen thought of the picture she had noticed on Jonah's desk, a close-up of a pretty blond-haired woman smiling at the camera. She wanted to ask how his wife died, though it clearly wasn't any of her business. But she needed to say something—anything—to fill the silence between them.

"It's hard not to admire Betty's enthusiasm," she said at last. "She doesn't seem timid, so that will be a plus in learning to skate. And now that I think about it, I'd like to teach her. But maybe it would be best if her first lesson took place at an indoor rink at the rec center."

"Are you sure?"

Probably not. In the years since the rape, she had done a lot to overcome the trauma—going through counseling, learning self-defense, becoming a police officer. But skating had always been the one hurdle that she hadn't been brave enough to face. She'd told herself it was okay, that hockey was a part of her past that was no longer relevant to her life today. But maybe it was finally time to confront that final demon. Besides, she had made the offer, and it seemed unfair to Betty to pull it back now.

She looked at Jonah and nodded. "Yeah. It's just that all of a sudden it hit me that going to the rink might stir up some things that are best left in the past. And for a moment there, I wasn't sure I was ready. But it's time to get past that, right?"

"That's your decision," Jonah said. "You haven't skated at all since moving away?"

She shook her head. "Being in LA made that part easy. It's not like Minnesota, where there's an outdoor rink at every park in the winter and a Zamboni in every rec center all year round." She took another deep breath. "But it will do me good to get back on the ice. All I need to do is find a pair of skates."

"Maybe someone in your family kept your old ones."

Carmen thought about that. It would have been nice, sweet even, if Lynn Trainor had tucked away any of her old hockey parapher-nalia after she left town. But her mother had never been sentimental. And the trailer was so small that there was little storage space for stuff like pads and equipment.

"Maybe," she said. "But if not, I'm sure I can pick up a pair at the Skate Exchange on Main."

"Hard to believe that a town this size has a whole store dedicated to hockey gear and skates."

"Typical Minnesota." Carmen's fingers reached for the door handle as the conversation seemed to be coming to a close. "It gets cold, and everyone starts to think hockey. And the meteorologists are saying it could dip below freezing tonight. But who knows? Seems like their predictions are wrong as much as they are right these days."

"Yeah," he agreed. "Listen. We spent all this time talking about Betty and skating, but you've said almost nothing about the guy who jumped you outside the gym."

She blew out a long sigh. "He was wearing a ski mask, so I couldn't see his face or hair. When he first came up behind me, he whispered something like, 'Can't you take a hint?' I assume that meant about giving up on the investigation into Sara's murder."

"You didn't recognize the voice?"

"No. Well, maybe. There was something

familiar there. But I still can't put my finger on it."

"It might come to you later when things have settled down. There must be some connection here to your cold case. Are any of the original suspects still in town?"

"There was really only one person of interest in the investigation. A guy by the name of Shane Rogan. He was actually a friend of my stepdad's. I think he lent a hand when he and my mom added a deck to their trailer."

"Was Rogan ever officially charged with the murder?"

"No. But from what I've read, he was a poster boy for bad decisions. The usual story—high-school dropout at fifteen, a trip to juvie after a number of drug busts and arrests for breaking and entering. He seemed to be turning things around when he became suspect number one in Sara's case. There was a lot of circumstantial evidence found at the murder site—an old T-shirt, some notes in his handwriting professing his love for Sara, who had been helping him work on his GED, an anonymous tip that placed him at the scene of the crime. The original thought was that Shane had made a move on Sara, and when she rebuffed him, he attacked and killed her. For a couple weeks, he really seemed good for it. He was hauled in for questioning, and the investigators did everything they could to wrangle a confession. But one by one, pieces of the case against him began to fall apart. In the end, the kid had a solid alibi, which the lead investigator couldn't shake. That should have been it then, but even after he was cleared of all charges, a lot of people in town continued to believe he had somehow gotten off on a technicality. Which explains why he moved off the grid to a cabin in the north woods."

"Did you reach out to him when you reopened the investigation?"

"I tried. But I never could get a good address for him. I had hoped Clint could help with that, but he claimed he didn't have any solid information."

"Well, until you discover this guy's whereabouts, you need to watch your back and be extra careful."

"That's the plan," she said, pushing open the car door and stepping onto the curb.

"If you don't mind, I'd like to walk you to your apartment," Jonah said.

She shrugged. "Okay."

As they walked toward the building, Jonah hurried to match her pace.

"When will Kirby move back in with you?"

"I have no idea. I still don't know where he is. At this point, all I can tell you is that he's spending some time with his dad. I've tried calling him, but he's not answering his phone."

"Why is that?"

"I have no idea." A shiver of panic ran up her spine. Nothing added up.

Except one thing. One name. One person. Shane Rogan.

And just like that, Carmen had an idea where Kirby and Clint were hiding out.

But she wasn't ready to share that information with Jonah.

EIGHT

Jonah gripped Betty's hand as they walked up the wide front steps of Foggy Falls Precinct 1. It was a rather grand name, considering it was the one and only police station in town. Still, the building had just the right amount of elegance to foster a bit of intimidation with its crenelated exterior and heavy wooden doors.

Betty was suitably impressed.

"It's like a castle," she said, pulling him forward up the short flight of stairs. "I'll be like a princess who likes to skate."

A prickle of anxiety darted down his back. A plan had been made to meet Carmen at the station and then proceed from there to the indoor rink. There was no turning back now that they were here. But was he about to make a colossal mistake?

The slight unease that had been brewing in the back of his mind had suddenly morphed into real concern. Someone out there was bent on hurting Carmen, and today's outing could potentially place his daughter in harm's way. And, if that wasn't enough, something else was bothering him as well, something related to his relationship with Carmen. Was it fair to Betty to encourage a friendship that was temporary at best? Was it fair to him?

He shook his head. Where had that question come from? A wave of guilt washed over him as he considered the possibility that a sense of loyalty to Julie's memory was keeping him from forging something more with Carmen. But Julie would never have wanted him to live in the past. She had always been all about embracing the possibilities of the future. He smiled as he imagined her taking him to task for falling into a rut of routine and predictability.

No. Julie wasn't the problem here. At least not the only one. It was his own guardedness and desire to avoid disappointment that was causing his insides to churn with hesitation. Maintaining the status quo had become his end game after Julie's death, and spending time with Carmen suddenly felt like a risk to that delicate balance.

"C'mon, Daddy!" Betty tugged on his arm. "Let's go find Carmen."

It was too late to reconsider. Carmen was expecting them, and even with all his trepidation, he had been looking forward to their little skating expedition as much as Betty. He pulled open the door to the station, willing away his natural wariness. He needed to enjoy the moment. Betty was happy, and that was the important thing. And learning to skate would be a skill that would serve her in good stead when the case was closed, and his family returned to the Twin Cities.

"There she is! Carmen, hi! We're here!" Betty waved a mittened hand and took off across the room, heading straight for Carmen.

Jonah took a step to follow when a lilting voice stopped him in his tracks. "Sorry. I know you're here to see one of our officers. But you still need to sign in."

"Sure. Sure." Jonah craned his neck to check on Betty. "I'm surprised they keep an admin here on Sunday afternoon."

"Oh, they don't usually. But—" the woman lowered her voice "—we're all-hands-on-deck after the bombing at the school. Course, you know all about that, don't you? You were the one who shouted out a warning just in time to save Carmen's life. It's scary for these officers who put their lives on the line every single day. I do what I can, but I'm just here to answer the phones."

"Don't listen to her," Carmen called from across the room. "Lisa basically keeps this whole place running. She puts in more hours than most of the staff. The station would fall apart if she wasn't here."

"Not true." Lisa blushed and looked away.

Jonah scrawled his name in the guest log and then headed over toward Carmen's desk. She must have been off the clock because, instead of her uniform, she was wearing a long green sweater over tapered jeans and boots.

"I know we're early." He shoved his hands in his pocket as an unfamiliar feeling of awkwardness descended between them. "But I've been dealing all morning with a very excited little girl."

Carmen looked up from her keyboard and shot him a smile. "Not a problem. I was just finishing some paperwork. Anyway, the rec center doesn't open until one, so we don't need to rush. Oh, and, Jonah. When I told the chief you would be coming by today, he said he'd like you to stop in his office for another little chat. I'm not sure what it's about, but I told him I'd pass on the request. I'd be glad to keep an eye on Betty."

"Fine," Jonah said. Maybe he could use

this "little chat" as an opportunity to find out more about the bombing.

He knocked on the chief's door, and a booming voice bid him to step inside.

"Thanks for coming by." Bill Tuttle's lips creased to form a smile. "I have a few things to say if you've got a couple minutes."

Jonah sat down in the same chair he had occupied last time and waited for the chief to explain.

"So…" Bill Tuttle rubbed his hand against his bald head. "Last time we spoke, I didn't have the chance to thank you for saving Carmen's life. The more I hear about what happened at the high school, the more I realize that if you hadn't taken such quick action, she might not be here with us today."

Jonah took a moment to consider this. In their past encounters, Bill Tuttle hadn't been nearly this polite. So why the sudden change of tone?

"I was glad to be in the right place at the right time," he said evenly. "Have you uncovered any motive for the bombing?"

"No. But we're not letting up, even for one minute."

"Glad to hear it. It's hard for me to imagine why anyone would want Carmen dead."

"After twenty years on the force, the one

thing I've learned for sure is that it's impossible to understand the criminal mind. People do bad things for good reasons, and vice versa. Well, that's all I wanted to say for now. If I think of any other questions, I'll be sure to give you a ring."

That was short and sweet. Jonah closed the door to the office and paused for a moment to consider what the chief had said at the end of their little chat. *If I think of any other questions, I'll be sure to give you a ring.*

You do that, he had felt like answering. Since when was he at Bill Tuttle's beck and call? It was gamesmanship, pure and simple, but tempting as it was, he wasn't about to pull rank and blow his cover.

"Hi, Dad," Betty called out from behind the reception desk. "Lisa is showing me a slideshow of pictures of cats. They're all so cute. Can we get a gray-and-white kitten, please?"

"This isn't something we need to talk about right now," Jonah said.

"But, Dad. Please. I really want a pet." Betty sighed dramatically as she scooted around the partition. She turned her sad face toward Lisa. "Sorry, I have to go now. But I liked looking at your pictures."

"Anytime, kid," Lisa said.

"Let me grab my skates," Carmen said,

coming up behind them to join the group by the front desk. "Then we can be off to the rink for Betty's first official lesson."

It brought a smile to his face, watching Betty skip off toward the car, clutching Carmen's hand. But thirty minutes later, he was regretting his part in the skating expedition.

Apparently, skate lacing, like every other part of parenting, called for a huge amount of patience, which, for Jonah, had always been a virtue that was in short supply. Betty didn't make it easy. She squirmed and arched her feet as he knelt on the cold, hard surface and attempted to adjust the fit of her rented skates.

"Too tight!" Betty wailed.

Jonah loosened her laces and tried again. The last time he had taken Betty skating, when they still lived in the Cities, the entire enterprise had been a disaster. At least this time around, when and if they ever made it onto the ice, he would be equipped with a good pair of skates. Following Carmen's recommendation, he had checked out the inventory at the Skate Exchange and found a pair that fit his size-eleven feet.

Carmen caught his glance at her own battered skates and smiled sheepishly. "Turned out my mom had kept mine from high school. The blades are dull, but they'll do for now."

Sharpened skates or not, Carmen was a rock star as she took a quick turn across the ice. Jonah tried to follow her, but that was proving to be impossible. Finally taking pity on him, Carmen slung an arm around his waist and demonstrated how to slide forward while pushing back with the opposite leg.

Betty, on the other hand, took to the ice like a fish to water. Of course, it helped that she had a chair to push along and help her keep her balance. Before they could stop her, she was wobbling away from them to the other side of the rink.

After watching his daughter for a few seconds, he turned to face Carmen. Big mistake. Even with his better-fitting skates, he still couldn't stop himself from falling yet again, his arms whirling like windmills to keep his balance. It did the trick for a few seconds before his left skate hit a bump on the ice, and his body crashed backward yet again.

Carmen was quick to offer encouragement. "Remember, you have to keep your shoulders and head forward."

Jonah grinned up at her from his sprawled position on the ice. "I think you're enjoying watching me fall."

Carmen stretched out her hand to help pull him up. "Sorry, Jonah," she said. "I know from experience that it's a lot harder than it looks. Considering this is only your second time on skates, you really are doing great. Honestly."

"Thanks, Carmen," he said as he linked arms with her and held on tight. Now, that was better. In fact, it felt just right.

Maybe if he wobbled just a little bit more, she'd hold on longer and not let him go.

Carmen felt happier than she had in a long time, being here at the rink with Jonah and Betty. It was nothing like what she had imagined when she thought about being surrounded by so many memories from her past. Playing her first pee-wee hockey games as a seven-year-old. Making the varsity team and having her mom, Clint and toddler Kirby cheering for her from the bleachers. Winning in the semifinals of the high-school championship her junior year. Those were good times. And then there were the harder moments. The pain of being thrust against the sideboards as the result of a dirty check. And the worst memory of all—telling her team and coach that she had played her last game.

It had been the middle of her senior year. At first, everyone had been supportive, assuring her that she just needed time and that, hopefully, she'd feel better soon. But it was a different tune when she explained that she wasn't changing her mind about quitting the team. All of the sympathetic platitudes shifted to accusatory whispers and veiled questions. Was she really going to let everyone down? It had almost broken her heart when she had skated off the ice that last day, away from the teammates who had been her closest companions most of her life, away from the dream of winning the state championship, away from the prospect of a full-ride scholarship to a Division I college.

She had prepared herself to feel a rush of emotion when she laced up her skates. But with the indoor dome decked out for open skate, the rink was filled with moms and dads, grandparents, boys and girls. There were no nets or playing lines. So, instead of reminding her of her competitive days, it harkened back to her earliest memory of skating—when her mom shuffled across the ice in worn boots holding her hand as she tried out her brand-new birthday present of five-dollar thrift-store skates. She could still recall the astonishment she had felt gliding across the frozen pond, her little hand gripping her mom's threadbare gloves. In the ensuing years of training and practice, she had forgotten about that. The wonder. The joy. And the trust.

"Do you think I'm too old or just too uncoordinated?" Jonah's question interrupted her musings.

Carmen laughed. "Neither. You're new to this. It takes practice."

"Yeah, that's what I keep trying to tell myself, but look at my kid. She hasn't fallen nearly as much. I'm going to be black-and-blue tomorrow."

"It's because she's so much smaller," Carmen answered seriously, even though she knew Jonah was just kidding around. "And she's holding on to a chair. It's easier to balance when your gravitational pull is less."

Jonah raised his eyebrows but didn't offer a comment.

"Are you ready to try again, on your own?" she asked.

"I think I'll just hang with you for a while. That is, if you don't mind?" She shook her head. "Good," he said, tucking his arm even more tightly through hers. "It feels a lot more secure this way. I thought Mace was exaggerating when he was singing your praises the other day. But now that I've seen you in action, I'm even more impressed. You must have been some hockey player."

Carmen had to fight the urge toward false modesty. "Yeah, I was."

"Seriously, Carmen. You really are amazing."

A flush of pleasure warmed her cheeks. It had been a long time since someone praised her ability on the ice or referred to anything she did as amazing. She looked up and met his eyes with a smile.

"If you don't stop with the compliments, I might be tempted to turn in my badge and get a job giving skating lessons to kids and adults."

"Sign me up as your first student," Jonah said, grinning back at her.

"Ha," she said, leaning in closer as she and Jonah moved across the ice in near perfect synchronicity. Was it really this easy, letting go of all her worries and fears and reveling in the moment?

It seemed so. A comfortable camaraderie fell between them as Jonah concentrated on staying upright as they made a third pass around the rink. Carmen finally let go of his arm so she could skate backward in front of him to offer advice and suggestions. But her eyes never strayed too far from Betty, who was giggling with a couple of newfound friends in the far corner of the rink.

"If I can skate on my own all the way over to Betty without falling, I'll count it as a success." Jonah's eyes were fixed downward as he stared at his feet.

"You can do it," Carmen said.

With painstaking slowness, he glided across the ice.

"Daddy! Daddy!" Betty stumbled forward, anxious to join him. "This is Kelsey and Kendall! Kelsey is four, like me. But Kendall is already five. And she doesn't need a chair to help her skate!"

Carmen headed over as well to join the new friends as Jonah went to greet their parents, who were standing on the sidelines nearby.

"So, would any of you like to learn how to skate backward?" Carmen crouched down so she was level with the girls. The tallest one nodded.

Carmen explained, "The key is to wiggle your bottom."

The three kids burst into laughter.

"Really! I'm not joking!" She pretended to be serious and put her hands on her hips. She twisted her mouth into a mock look of sternness before swaying away from the girls, skating backward.

Her simple feat was met with enthusiastic cheers.

"I want to try, too," Betty said.

"All right, if you take turns and hold my hand, I can show all of you how to do it." Carmen skated back to the kids. She glanced over at Jonah, but he seemed engrossed in his conversation with the parents of the girls. He had thrown back his head and was laughing at something the tall, blonde woman was saying to the group. Above the rink, the scoreboard flickered on and off as the technician behind the glass barrier tested the system.

Home Team: 3. Visitors: 0.

How was it possible that it was the exact score of her very last game? Just like that, all of the hurt and rejection she had felt twelve years ago flooded her body, and a pang of loneliness thrummed in her chest. She was an outsider now, just as she had become after she left the team. The rush of feelings was so unexpected that, for a moment, she was afraid she might start crying. But she wasn't going to allow that. It was inevitable that she would be overcome with emotion being back in her old stomping grounds, but that was part of the past. It wasn't like she could feel lonely for something that didn't exist. A championship victory. A romantic relationship.

Huh? A tug on her arm reminded her that she needed to get back to the task at hand.

"Okay, I'm ready. Let's give it a try!" She injected some extra playfulness into her voice. And, as was so often the case, by pretending to be having a good time, she began to enjoy herself again. The girls didn't complain, even when they fell. And by the time ten minutes had elapsed, Kendall could skate a good twenty meters backward, while Kelsey and Betty could make it a few paces holding her hand.

"Daddy! You have to come here and see me!" Betty's imperious tone seemed to stir the other three adults from their conversation.

In hindsight, Carmen recognized that she should have anticipated what happened next. But in the moment, all she could do was watch in horror as Betty, eager to show off, pushed off against the ice by herself.

At first, it seemed as if she would be able to do it. Her first two strides sent her backward, but then her shoulders overextended, and her body tumbled to the ice. Jonah moved quickly to the rescue, clearly not expecting Betty to land in front of him as his blades slid ever closer to her prone form. Just in time, he managed to bring his skates to a full stop, though his body continued its trajectory forward as he landed with a thud on top of Betty.

Carmen was beside them in seconds. "Anybody hurt?"

"Yes!" Betty's cry was agonizing.

"I'm sorry, hon," Jonah said as he rubbed his knee.

"You fell on top of me." Betty's tone was high and accusatory.

"I know. I didn't mean to. I tried to stop. Can you tell me what hurts?"

"My ankle." Betty pointed to her left leg.

Carmen bent down to inspect the injury. Gently, she undid the laces of the skate and pulled the stocking foot out. The limb felt warm even through the layers of clothing, and she could measure the thickness around the ankle. "It may only be a sprain, but I can't be sure."

Jonah was still rubbing his knee as he shook his head.

"Can we help?" The two parents of Betty's new friends joined them.

"No." His voice was curt. "Thank you. But we can manage from here."

A wave of guilt washed over her. This was her fault. Why did she have to be such a show-off? She should have kept the focus on the basics instead of demonstrating more advanced moves. She sneaked a glance at Jonah's face as he unlaced his skates. Anxiety and regret clouded his countenance as he lifted Betty in his arms and carried her off the rink.

It was a painful drive to the urgent care center on the outskirts of town, punctuated with a great deal of moaning and groaning from Betty in the back seat.

"I just hope it won't be a long wait," Jonah said after a particularly loud scream of pain.

Happily, it wasn't. Before they had even finished checking in with the receptionist, a physicians' assistant appeared and motioned for them to follow her to the back.

"I'll wait here," Carmen said as her two companions disappeared behind the closed door. Jonah didn't even turn and acknowledge her response. Clearly, she was no longer part of the team. She ought to have followed her instincts and taken an Uber back to her apartment, but at the time, she had thought she could help with Betty. Now she was stuck here in the waiting room, feeling like a third wheel.

Cry me a river, as her mom used to say.

She paced back and forth across the large open space, with nothing to do but wallow in her thoughts.

Okay, fine, she told herself with a firm shake of the head. *You should have seen this coming. What made you think your presence would be welcome at this particular moment in time?* Jonah was in crisis mode, and Betty was too upset to consider anything but her own pain. Skating lessons were one thing, but accompanying the family to the urgent care center was a whole other matter. Apparently, she really didn't know her place.

Story of her life. She would always be the kid from the trailer park with the hand-me-down clothes. The girl who had the skills to skate with the boys but was invisible off the rink. The star hockey player who let down the team.

She'd thought Jonah was different. She thought he understood that feeling of being the odd one out and in need of a friend.

Apparently not. Unlike her, he had a normal life. A house. A child.

And she had… Bruno. But not for long, if the people at Foster Friends had anything to say about it.

Another stroll across the floor and she was back at the reception desk, startled to see her frowning face in the mirror, complete with smeared mascara, disheveled hair and a mis-buttoned cardigan bunched under her shoulder.

Ugh. How embarrassing.

"Is there a ladies' room nearby?"

The receptionist pointed a finger down the hall. "First door on the left," she said.

Five minutes later, face washed, hair combed and sweater correctly buttoned, Carmen felt ready to rejoin the human race. She was halfway through the bathroom door when a familiar voice stopped her in her tracks.

"Do you need to see my provider card?"

It sounded like… Could it be… Mr. Mace?

She stepped back across the threshold and peered through a crack in the door. She could just barely see the profile of the man standing in front of the reception desk.

Tall and bulky, with a head of thick gray hair. She had only a partial view of his face, but yup. It was Max Mace all right.

She let the door swing closed another half inch. The last thing she wanted was for him to catch sight of her lurking in the hall.

But Mace's focus didn't falter as he walked across the room and reached for a black North Face windbreaker hanging on the wall. As he turned to speak again to the receptionist, the mirror behind the desk caught the reflection of a white surgical patch covering his left eye.

Carmen sucked in a gasp as the attack outside the gym replayed in her mind and her brain connected the dots.

The voice. The clothing. And now the injured eye.

In the exact spot she had jammed her key.

NINE

Jonah lifted a sleepy-eyed Betty off the examination table. She yawned and stretched out her arms as he carried her through the hallway and into the reception area, where Carmen was waiting. Just for a moment, he had worried she might have gotten tired and gone home, but no. There she was, sitting on one of the chairs, looking even more upset than he was about the accident.

"Is everything okay?" he asked.

She fixed him with a wan smile. "Shouldn't I be asking you that?"

"Right. Well, then. I'm happy to report that everything's just fine now that all the screaming and crying is over. According to the doc, it's a stress fracture, and Betty will probably only need to wear the cast for four weeks or less. Apparently, kids' bones heal remarkably fast. And—" he paused to make sure his daughter was listening "—you'll be pleased to hear that this little girl was very brave."

"Proud of you, kiddo," Carmen said.

"Will you sign my cast?" Betty asked. "The doctor already drew a smiley face on the bottom, but there's plenty of room left for you…and Dad…and Grandma…and…" Her words trailed off as she closed her eyes and snuggled down against his shoulder.

"Can you believe it? Talking one minute and half asleep the next. The kid's like a race car that goes from zero to one hundred in five seconds flat and then back to zero again just like that. But how can I complain now that the screaming has stopped? Too bad it was such a dramatic ending to our skating adventure."

As they made their way through the front door and into the parking lot, Jonah adjusted Betty's position in his arms and struggled to match Carmen's rapid pace.

"I was in such a hurry to get us in to see the doctor that I didn't even think about the fact that I had left you waiting in the reception area. I just couldn't wrap my head around the fact that I'd caused the accident. I should have been paying better attention and reacted quicker when she fell in front of me."

"Everything happened so fast," Carmen said, opening the door and climbing into the car. "I just hope this doesn't put her off skating in the future."

"I doubt that, particularly if you're still willing to be her teacher."

A forced-looking smile was Carmen's only response.

He buckled Betty into her car seat and slid in behind the wheel. "Shall I take you back to your apartment?"

"Could you drop me at the station? I picked up my car this morning, so I don't want to leave it overnight in the lot."

"Sure." Jonah shifted his eyes sideways toward the passenger seat. What was going on with Carmen? Her voice seemed flat, and her eyes were fixed straight ahead. Was it possible that she was blaming herself for Betty's accident?

No. It was perfectly obvious it was his fault. It had to be something else making her so upset.

They drove along in silence, and by the time they reached the station, Betty was sound asleep. Carmen leaned forward, preparing to get out.

"Thanks for the ride. I..." Her voice trailed off.

"Carmen. Seriously. What's wrong?"

"Nothing. Well, not nothing. It's just

that…" She folded her hands and looked down at her lap. "I wasn't going to mention this because you have so much else on your plate. But I saw Mr. Mace at the urgent care. He was wearing the same kind of jacket as the man who attacked me Friday night. And his eye was covered in the spot where I poked the attacker with my key."

Jonah cut the ignition and swiveled to face her. "Wait. Are you saying Mace was the one who assaulted you outside the gym?"

She nodded. "I'm sure of it. And now that I think about it, I realize why I thought his voice was so familiar. It was high, almost a falsetto, just like the fake tone Mace would use to cheer on the team."

He took a deep breath. "What did he say when he saw you?"

"That's the thing, Jonah. He didn't see me. At least I don't think he did. I was coming out of the bathroom when I heard his voice, and I stepped back inside so I wouldn't have to talk to him. I was afraid he would say something about Kirby, and I didn't want to have that conversation." She shook her head. "I'm sorry to add yet another crazy element to the day's events, but I had this sick feeling in my stomach when I saw his black windbreaker. And it got worse when I saw the patch."

Jonah settled back against his seat and considered this, anger and outrage coursing through his veins. "So, Mace is your mystery assailant."

He meant it as a statement, but Carmen seemed to have inserted a question mark at the end of his words.

"You don't believe me," she said.

"Quite the opposite. Our esteemed assistant principal has been on my radar for quite some time. I noticed right away that he seemed to have a finger in every pie around the school, and more times than I can count, I've seen him in a deep conversation with one of the students I suspect of using. But what happened to cause him to come after you?"

Carmen raised her shoulders in a half shrug. "I don't know what to say."

Betty stirred suddenly with a soft sound somewhere between a murmur and a sigh. Jonah glanced into the back seat. But just as quickly, she nodded back off to sleep.

"Okay," he said after a minute. "I'm going to have to think about this and see if I can figure out our next move. The one thing I know for sure is that you need to be careful. Something like this cannot happen again. If Mace didn't see you at the clinic, he probably feels safe. But there's always the chance that he did spot you in the hallway but decided to remain mum. If that's true, then you become an even bigger threat because you can identify him as your attacker. And you can press charges, even if they don't stick. This drug operation in Foggy Falls represents a lot of easy money to the people involved, which means any one of the major players will stop at nothing to avoid detection. I just don't understand why. Unless…" He paused. "Unless it has something to do with Kirby."

Carmen's voice trembled. "Please, God. No."

"I hope it's not true. But you need to accept the possibility that your brother has gotten in over his head. I told you how Mace had been pushing me to press charges after the incident in the cafeteria. I'm just thinking out loud here, but maybe Kirby knows something about Mace's operation. That would explain why Mace would want to sideline him, at least for the time being. And maybe by threatening you, he's sending a signal that Kirby needs to stay mum about what's going on at the school."

"There's a lot of speculation involved in that theory," Carmen said.

"Maybe so. But the important thing is that you don't take any chances until we can figure this out." Jonah pulled in a deep breath as he recalled the sight of Carmen, her mouth set in a determined frown, chasing her hooded attacker. Though beaten and bruised, she was still unbroken, and the recollection of that moment pulled at some forgotten place in his heart.

He shook off that memory and forced himself to focus on the situation at hand. "And Kirby is still keeping a low profile, somewhere out of town?"

Carmen nodded.

"Good. Well, at least we know he's safe. I just wish we could find him so we could ask about Mace."

She seemed to be considering her words carefully before reaching a decision. "I did have an idea about that," she said. "Do you remember me telling you about that guy, Shane Rogan, who was the main suspect in Sara's murder? He and Clint were pretty tight back in the day, so it occurred to me that Kirby and Clint may have gone up north to stay with him. But without an address or any contact information, I wasn't able to follow up on that."

"Is it possible that your mom knows more than she's saying?"

"Maybe."

Betty opened her eyes and kicked her leg with the cast against the front seat. "I'm hungry, Daddy. Do you think when we get home Grandma will make me some mac and cheese?"

"Absolutely, hon. I'm sure she'd be glad to." He turned back toward Carmen. "I suppose I should take Betty home for dinner. Let's talk tomorrow. If you could somehow pressure your mom into giving you an address for this Shane character, maybe we could fly up there for a little meet and greet. Classes resume tomorrow, but I could take a day off sometime during the week. Kill two birds with one stone. I could ask Kirby about Mace, and you could question Rogan about Sara Larssen."

"This is really hard for me, Jonah. I know Kirby has been taking drugs for a while now, and I can't get past the fact that I wasn't here to help him. And despite what you say, I can't imagine he knows much more beyond the next place to get his stash. It's heartbreaking to believe there's more to this than that."

"Maybe not. But it's possible he recognized the danger, and that's why he ran away. Which makes me think you need to watch your back every minute. And remember. No one on the police force is to be trusted. No one, Carmen, not even the chief."

Carmen's countenance revealed her dismay.

"Daddy," came a plaintive whine from the back seat. "I want to go home."

"Listen. I've got to get Betty back to the house before there's another major meltdown. But I don't think you should return to your place. Why don't you spend a few days with us, at least until we can get some answers?"

Carmen shook her head. "Thanks for the offer, but I can stay with my mom. I'm thinking that while I'm there, I might be able to talk her into giving me an address for Shane Rogan."

Carmen watched the taillights of Jonah's car disappear out of the parking lot before fishing her keys out of her pocket. The tension was back in her neck, and her shoulders were tight from the strain of the day. It was a pity, because everything had started out so optimistically, with Betty eager and excited, and Jonah friendly and lighthearted, glad to have company for the adventure ahead. They hadn't talked about drugs or her murder case, instead just focusing on the trip to the ice rink. And it had been fun and unexpectedly thrilling to strap on her skates and glide across the ice like old times.

But of course, everything had gone pear-shaped even before Betty's fall. And seeing Mace at the urgent care center had rattled her more than she wanted to admit. But it was Jonah's not-so-subtle attempt to tie Kirby to Mace and the drugs that was most worrisome. Not that anything Jonah had said about Kirby came as a surprise. His conclusions were logically drawn, but it was a line of thinking that she hadn't let her own mind go down.

She twirled her keys in her hand, her fingers touching the well-worn metal keychain that had been given to her by a friend at her old church in LA. Just brushing her thumb across the engraving was enough for the words from the book of Joshua to flash into her head. *Be strong and courageous. Do not be discouraged, for the Lord your God will be with you wherever you go.* She rubbed the flat metal rectangle once more and then heaved a sigh before clicking the unlock button and opening the door to her car.

Maybe it was time to confront her mom and demand some answers. Surely, she knew where Kirby and Clint were hiding out. But that didn't mean her mom would tell her. She could almost guarantee her mom would become defensive and very possibly send her off on a wild-goose chase.

Carmen drummed her fingers against the steering wheel. The thought of initiating that particular confrontation filled her with dread. A pit tightened in her stomach. She really did not want to go home.

Home. Was the trailer her home? The twenty-five-by-fifty-foot double-wide where she had been raised? It was certainly the place she had lived in the longest, but it didn't feel like her home. Not anymore. Neither did the apartment she was currently renting or even her cozy little studio in LA. Her aunt's place, where she had gone to stay after she left high school, felt most like home. Maybe. Her aunt had been kind, and at least there she hadn't felt either completely alone or unwanted. But she was beginning to realize that she had never lived in a real home like the one Jonah shared with Betty and Elizabeth.

She tapped the brakes as she approached the intersection at Harbor and Ninth before flicking on her blinker and making a left turn. She had told Jonah she would stay at the trailer park with her mom, but first there were a few things at her apartment she needed to collect—a change of clothes, her laptop and, most importantly, Bruno. What would her mom think of that? Actually, she'd probably be fine hosting a rescue dog. She'd always had a soft spot for animals. Not that they'd had any pets growing up. There was hardly room for two adults and two kids in the cramped double-wide. But Mom would probably be quite welcoming to Bruno. She couldn't say the same for the reception she herself would receive.

Dusk was already falling when she pulled into the parking lot and turned off the engine. During her time out west, she had never quite gotten used to the long hours of sunshine and warmth. No doubt, by the time February rolled around, she would be wishing for longer days, but there was something satisfying and comforting about the dark.

As she opened the car door and stepped outside, a cold wind whipped against her neck and hair. *Brrr.* The air felt heavy, like it might start to snow at any moment. Maybe she'd better grab her winter jacket from the closet as well. She trudged through the lobby and then up the stairs. As she opened the door, a blur of white-and-tan fur rushed toward her, and she squatted down to greet Bruno. She stroked behind his ears, and his tail thumped behind him. She could feel the beginnings of a smile forming on her lips. This might not feel quite like her home, at least not yet, but it sure was nice to have someone waiting to welcome her when she walked through the door.

She was about to stand up and start collecting her things when she noticed that Bruno's tail had abruptly stopped wagging, and his ears were pricked forward. Her hand froze against his fur as goosebumps shot down her arms, a sudden awareness flashing through her brain. Without glancing behind her at the still open door, she flung herself forward, over Bruno, rolling into a somersault, and then sprang to her feet and dashed across the kitchen toward her bedroom.

She didn't have to look behind her to know that an intruder had broken into the apartment as the thud of footsteps echoed her tread. How could she have been so stupid? Regrets barraged her brain, even as her hand closed around the base of a lamp, which she hurled behind her. It was beyond foolish not to have closed and locked the door, especially after what had happened at the gym. Even worse, she had known that Mace may have seen her at the hospital, but she had naively thought he wouldn't come after her in her own home.

If she could only reach her bedroom, she could retrieve the extra Glock she kept beside her bed.

Bang!

A bullet exploded behind her, and without thinking, she dove to the left, just as another whizzed across the room, shattering a picture on the wall. It had been taken at her mom and Clint's wedding and showed a chubby, freckled, two-year-old Kirby holding both of her hands as they twirled in circles on the dance floor. She had been fifteen at the time, but she could still feel the joy and excitement she had felt to have a new brother and dad.

She stared at the broken glass for what felt like a minute as anger exploded in her chest. Her childhood might not have been filled with happy memories, but there were still a few littered along the way. How dare someone take that away. Blood and adrenaline surged through her body as she hurled herself behind the sofa and another bullet blasted through the air.

Her mind registered the clamor of footsteps approaching the spot where she was hiding. She waited a moment and held her breath. Just a little closer. Now!

She pushed against the couch with all her might and felt it connect against the leg of her assailant. A mumbled curse was followed by the thud of a body falling. Without pausing to think, she threw herself back over the sofa, on top of the man scrambling to regain his footing.

He was short and burly, approximately midtwenties. Not Mace then, though it was more than possible this was someone who had been hired to do Mace's bidding. But now wasn't the time to stop and interrogate the intruder, not until she managed to disarm and disable him. Momentarily stunned by her counterattack and the unexpected weight pinning him down, the man didn't resist as her hands closed around his right arm. A moment later, his fingers released their grip on the pistol, and it slid across the floor.

She was about to make a dive for it when the sounds of Bruno's frantic barking cut through her awareness. She froze for a moment and glanced briefly at her dog. Bruno's head was out the door, and his body looked tight with tension. There was a growl to his bark that she had never heard before.

And then she heard the ding of the elevator. Panic swamped her brain. Someone was about to come down the hall. Someone who might be able to help her. Or, even more likely, someone working with her attacker.

Her hands flexed forward to find the nearest object within reach. A portable radio. Not ideal, but it was the best she could do on the spur of the moment. She snatched the boom box and smashed it down on the man's head. Scrambling upright and unable to spot the fallen pistol, she sprinted out the door, with Bruno following close behind her. The elevator was to her right, but the better choice seemed to be the stairwell on the far side of the building.

Her heart pumped even harder as she charged toward the stairs. She dared a glance behind her. Bruno had been right to be so tense. A man even larger than the one she had left in her apartment was right behind her.

Her breaths were coming in pants as she threw open the door to the stairwell. Gripping the railings on both sides, she thrust her body forward and slid down the first flight of stairs. She turned the corner to the second flight as she heard the door above her open. Again, she used her arms to slide forward, carrying her body faster than her feet could.

She flung the door to the lobby open and was sprinting toward the exit when she saw a third man leaning lazily against the door.

Carmen froze, her mind scrambling. She was surrounded. She changed direction toward a wall of windows. Dare she throw herself through the glass? She was preparing to take the risk when the main door to the apartment building swung open. And the little hope she had for escape shriveled in her chest. One against one were odds she could handle. One against three was a bit less promising. But one against six seemed impossible.

And now three more men were about to enter the building.

TEN

Run!

Her legs felt frozen as her eyes fixed on the men entering through the front door, and her throat constricted in an audible gasp. These men were no strangers. She would know that mop of wild curls pushed back by a black headband anywhere. But how was it possible? Could it really be…her family? Her gaze flitted from Kirby to Clint and to a third guy she didn't know. Confusion and wonder ballooned in her chest. Her odds of escape had just increased exponentially. But these weren't trained fighters. They were unarmed civilians in harm's way. Relief and anxiety crowded her brain.

Her heart skipped a beat as one of the brutes behind her raised his weapon and pointed it at Kirby.

"No!" she screamed as she took off running.

The gunman seemed to hesitate as Clint came barreling toward him.

Anger, fear and love jangled together in her head. There was no way she could reach the shooter in time to save her brother. And Clint wasn't fast enough either. Despair wound around her heart even as her legs kept pumping her forward, her eyes locked on the pistol.

Grrrr. Grrr. A low growl broke through her concentration as a blur of furry ferocity propelled past her.

Bruno.

"Yowl! Augh!" The man howled with surprise as the little dog sank his teeth into his leg. The distraction gave Clint just enough time to tackle the shooter and wrestle his gun from his hand.

Carmen's gait slowed as it seemed for a moment that the danger had passed. But only for a moment.

"Carmen! Watch out!" The shout came from Kirby.

The two men from upstairs streamed through the stairwell door, pistols at the ready.

"We need to get out of here!" Carmen cried.

Kirby and his companion took off through the door as Clint fired two rounds at the men behind them.

Grabbing Clint's arm, Carmen pulled him through the exit. Her eyes darted to the left and right. Which way to go? If only she had her keys, but she'd left them on the table.

"Get in," Clint cried as his rusty old F-150 skidded toward them, with Kirby at the wheel and the mystery man in the passenger seat next to him.

She and Clint jumped into the truck, and Kirby took off, burning rubber as he headed down the road.

"Bruno!" Carmen cried.

"I've got him right here." The man in the front turned to face her. "Hey. I'm Shane. Shane Rogan." He stretched an arm down toward the floor, lifted the little pup up and handed him to Carmen.

Relief—and confusion—flooded her senses. Bruno was safe. But what was Shane Rogan doing with Clint and Kirby? And why was Kirby the one driving?

"Kirby! What are you doing? You don't have a license."

"I had a permit for a while until I got suspended. But why are you freaking out? I can get us where we're going as well as any of these other guys."

"Hey," Clint said.

"Right. Except for Dad," Kirby added.

Okay, okay. Enough chitchat. She needed to marshal her thoughts and make a plan. The neighbors had probably called 911 to report the shooting. And, at this point, the intruders had probably taken off. Which meant they ought to head back to the crime scene and give a statement.

"Kirby! You need to turn around and go back to the apartment. I need to report the break-in to the police."

"I'm not doing that. I don't want to talk to the cops, and neither do Dad and Shane. And you shouldn't want that either, considering all the stuff that's been happening around here."

She turned sideways in her seat to focus her appeal on the most mature member of the trio of rescuers. "Clint, we really do need to go back."

"Sorry, kid. Kirby's not wrong when he says that none of us want to talk to police. We've all experienced more than our fair share of police harassment. And who knows how they would spin our arrival just now. We didn't do anything wrong, but I'm sure Tuttle would be dubious of our timing." He paused and then added in a softer tone, "What was going on back there? Why were those three men after you?"

She wasn't about to tell him about Mace.

There was already too much bad blood there. Besides, what could she say? For all she knew, the men waiting for her at the apartment had no connection to the assistant principal. It was possible. Just not likely.

"It may have something to do with Sara Larssen's murder," she said at last.

A satisfied smile spread across Clint's face. "Well, maybe we can help you with that. But it will have to wait until we get back to the trailer."

"The trailer? No. What are you talking about? Clint! You need to tell Kirby to go back to the apartment. We need to…"

"No can do, kid," Clint replied. "Now, settle back and enjoy the ride. It will all be explained to you shortly."

Her only other choice being to fling her body out the door of a moving vehicle, Carmen closed her eyes and cradled Bruno to her chest, trying hard not to think about the consequences of leaving the scene without filing a report.

Finally, with the crunch of gravel, Kirby pulled into the loose-stone drive and led the way into the trailer.

One by one, they walked inside. Carmen pulled out a chair and joined the three men at the tiny dining-room table. No one spoke for a minute, until Carmen's impatience got the best of her. "So, are you ready to tell me why you were at my apartment?"

"We came to tell you what we found inside the little free library," Kirby said.

"Little free library? What are you talking about?"

"At Sara's house," Shane added for clarification.

Suddenly, Carmen remembered spotting the small book house on the Larssen property when she had gone to get a closer look at the crime scene. But surely the investigators had checked the structure for any evidence relating to the murder.

Clint shook his head. "Maybe we should start at the beginning, back when Kirby and I drove up to see my old buddy Shane. So, the three of us were sitting around, sharing a pizza, and…"

Impatience gnawed at Carmen's gut. Clint seemed to be relishing the suspense of the story. But she knew from experience there was no way of fast-forwarding him to the end.

"Anyway," Clint continued. "The conversation took a turn, and Shane started talking about how the cops tried to frame him for that teacher's murder. It's old news, but we were all in agreement that it was beyond ridiculous."

Shane nodded. "I told the cops I wasn't a violent guy, but they didn't want to listen."

"The police have to follow every lead," Carmen explained. "And they did find your T-shirt at the scene of the murder."

"I'd spilled coffee on it during my last tutoring session with Sara. I explained that, but they didn't care. They claimed they had an anonymous tip from someone who could place me at the cabin on the day of the murder."

"Mace." Kirby spit out the name like it was poison. "Mace was their so-called witness."

Carmen blinked, surprised. "Do you know that for a fact?"

"That's the thing, Carmen," Clint answered her with a sad smile. "We know lots of stuff, but that doesn't mean we have any evidence. It's called intuition. Gut feeling. You're a cop, and we respect that. But someone botched the investigation ten years ago and tried to blame Shane. So forgive me if I don't trust anyone but you."

"Sara was a good person who didn't deserve to die," Shane spoke up, again in a voice that was soft but sure. "She was helping me get my life back on track by tutoring me in

English and math. And leaving me books in the little library I helped her build in front of her place. When she showed me a picture of what it was supposed to look like, I asked her why she wanted me to make a birdhouse on stilts." He laughed at the memory. "But she explained that she wanted people walking by her cabin to be able to exchange an old book for a new one. That way they would always have something to read. Then she had this idea that we should leave a thin space between the plywood on the roof where she could slip in a note about an assignment for me. I had almost forgotten about that with everything that happened after the murder. But when we got to talking, I started to wonder if she left one last note in the hidden slot. So we drove down to the cabin, and I pushed aside the top panel and looked inside."

"And…" Carmen prompted.

"There was no note, no message." Shane's lips quirked in a grin. "Just an old Motorola Razr."

"What? How did the investigators miss that?" Carmen mentally reviewed the cold-case file. No mention of a hidden slot. Nor was there any reference to a cell belonging to Sara Larssen that had been recovered at the scene. Could this at long last be the missing phone?

Clint shrugged. "Who knows? Weren't they all semi-incompetent?"

"No," Carmen said. She was about to say more when Shane interrupted.

"No matter how you look at it, finding the phone is a game changer. Of course, the battery was dead. And naturally, we couldn't find a charger, being that it's so old. But still. What if there's some kind of message on the phone that would help catch Sara's killer?"

"Let's not get ahead of ourselves here," Carmen said. Much as she hoped this could be a huge break in her case, she was reluctant to jump to conclusions. "It may turn out that the phone doesn't even belong to Sara."

"It's Sara's, all right," Shane said. "Hers had a half dozen scratches on the front part of the cover, exactly like the one we found."

Carmen pulled in a deep breath. "Where is this Motorola Razr right now?"

Shane pulled it from the back pocket of his jeans and set it on the table.

Four sets of eyes stared at the battered blue flip phone. Then the three men around the table trained their glances on Carmen.

"Okay," she said. She was struggling to remain calm in light of such a potential break.

"I assume all of you have touched it." Three nods. "Okay. Maybe at this point it's putting the cart before the horse, but I'm going to grab a plastic bag and try to preserve what's left of its integrity."

Clint leaned back in his chair, a pleased grin creasing the corners of his mouth. "See, guys. I told you she'd be interested. As soon as Shane mentioned the hidden compartment, I was like, whoa, maybe there's a clue in there."

"Sara had a boyfriend, you know." Shane's voice was little more than a whisper. "I think it was that guy Mace."

Carmen slipped the phone into a plastic bag she had found in a kitchen drawer. "Did Sara tell you they were dating?"

"No. It was more a feeling I had from the stuff Mace said when I saw him in town. I know it sounds crazy, but it almost seemed like he was jealous of the time I was spending with Sara."

A palpable excitement pounded in Carmen's veins. If Mace killed Sara, it made sense that he would try to set up Shane as a convenient scapegoat. And, as the years passed, Mace must have felt confident that he had gotten away with the crime.

Carmen pushed her chair back from the

table and made a move toward the door. "I need to pay a quick visit to a friend who has been helping with the case. Actually, Kirby, he's someone you already know. Mr. Drake? The teacher you stabbed with a pen?"

Kirby rolled his eyes. "Don't remind me."

"Clint, can I borrow your truck to drive back into town?"

"I'm coming with you," Kirby said, pulling his keys from his pocket. "After seeing those guys who were waiting for you at the apartment, I don't think you should be on your own."

"Okay," Carmen agreed. "But I want to drive."

The traffic in front of the high school was moving at a snail's pace.

In the passenger seat of his Subaru, Jonah tapped his fingers against his knees as Elizabeth inched along in the line. He needed to curb his impatience. Lending his mother-in-law his car while hers was in the shop was such a small sacrifice, especially considering everything she had done for him. Besides, they wouldn't be running so late if it wasn't for Betty's dillydallying.

Minor annoyances didn't usually bother him. But they did today. He was wired and exhausted, unable to think in a coherent way. Last night's visit from Carmen and Kirby had left him feeling confused and un-moored. When they arrived at his door at a little past eight thirty, he had been about to get Betty settled down in her bed. He had been surprised to see Carmen, but not dismayed. But then came the news that she had been attacked at her apartment and that Kirby and his friends had discovered evidence that could potentially break open her case.

But as he processed all the information, Jonah felt his worlds begin to collide. His worries about Betty and Elizabeth and his determination to shield them from the dangers of his job. His obligations as an officer of the law, especially now that the chain of custody for important evidence had been violated. And, as a final complication, those confusing feelings related to his friendship with Carmen and his desire to protect her from the people who wanted her dead.

But so far, he hadn't done a very good job of it.

It hurt his brain just to think about it. There had been too many incidents where Carmen had barely escaped with her life.

The only way to stop the attacks was to put the thugs behind bars. To that end, he'd wanted to commandeer the phone and send it to the BCA. But without breaking his cover, he hadn't been able to offer any reasonable explanation to Kirby for why he should take possession of the phone. "Finders, keepers," Kirby had replied to his offer to look at the evidence. There was definitely still a degree of animosity between him and the teenager. At least Carmen had agreed that handing the evidence over to the Foggy Falls forensic team wasn't a viable solution. The last group of investigators had bungled the case, and it was hard to trust that it wouldn't happen again. So, over his strong protests and despite a vigorous debate, the phone remained in the hands of the trio who'd found it.

With Betty tugging on his arm, demanding yet another story, he had somehow extracted a promise that the phone would be handled with the utmost care until they were able to authenticate the ownership. Hardly a great plan, but a compromise nonetheless. He'd even gone so far as to suggest that Carmen and Kirby call on Sandy Coltrane, the science teacher at the high school. She'd helped him once when he'd had trouble connecting his old router, and he'd seen firsthand the vast collection of audiovisual equipment she had amassed in her basement. Whatever Sandy's reasons for accumulating her collection, she was their best chance at finding a charger that fit the phone.

But now, in the cold light of morning, it seemed reckless to have allowed such a pivotal piece of evidence to remain in the hands of civilians. What had he been thinking? Truth be told, in the moment, he wasn't thinking. His mind had been occupied with the image of Carmen being chased through her apartment building. On balance, the new piece of evidence seemed much less important, though that was certainly not the correct reaction for a law enforcement officer. He needed to get his emotions in check and not allow worries about Carmen to distract him.

Given all the drama of the day before, it wasn't surprising that sleep had been hard to come by as he tossed and turned in his bed. No wonder he was such a grump this morning, snapping at Betty when she refused to get dressed and tuning out his mother-in-law's advice about the traffic.

Now he truly was going to be late. He glanced down at his watch and winced. It was almost eight o'clock, and the line of vehicles in front of the school didn't seem to be moving.

"Look at the back of that car," Betty said,

clamoring for attention from the back seat. "It has a picture of four people and a dog on the window."

"I see it, sweetheart." Elizabeth turned to face Jonah. "Are you sure you don't want to get out and walk? I don't want you to be late for your class."

Jonah shook his head. "We're almost there."

Three minutes later, Elizabeth pulled up in front of the school. Jonah was reaching down to unbuckle his seat belt when a tall man in a navy sports jacket and khaki pants stepped in front of the car.

Mace.

How had he forgotten that the assistant principal liked to be front and center to welcome late arrivals?

Jonah pushed open the passenger door and stepped out on the curb. But before Elizabeth could take her leave, Mace tucked his fingers into a fist and knocked on the hood of the Subaru.

Frowning, Elizabeth rolled down the window.

Mace stuck his head into the car and boomed his greeting. "Hi there, Drake family. How are all of you today?"

"Great!" Betty chirped, leaning forward

in her car seat for a better view. "Except for my hurt leg."

Mace peered in for a closer look. "That's a mighty impressive cast you have there, young lady. Did you take a tumble while chasing your grandma around the house?"

"No." Betty giggled. "Dad stepped on my leg while we were skating at the ice rink with Carmen."

"That sounds painful. You know, now that I think about it, I thought I saw your dad's car at the urgent care yesterday afternoon. Did Carmen come along to help when you went to the doctor?"

"Yes. She signed my cast. You can, too, if you have a marker."

"Sure. I'd love to." He straightened up and pulled a Sharpie from his jacket pocket. "Hmm. What should I say? Oh, I know." A minute passed as he scribbled a note. When he finished, he kept his head still tucked inside the car. "Well, I'm glad I got to visit with all of you today. Any big plans for the afternoon? Maybe more special time with Grandma?"

"Um, I guess." Betty's forehead pleated in confusion.

"Well, whatever you do, you need to be careful. Look what happened while you were skating with Carmen. And she certainly knows her way around the ice. Did you know that I used to coach her when she played hockey?"

"Did you coach her brother, too?"

"Kirby? No. He never showed an interest, though he might have been quite a good skater. Do you know him, too?"

"Not really. I met him yesterday when he came over with Carmen to talk to my dad. He seemed nice."

Elizabeth's hand reached down and slid the gear shift into Drive. "Excuse us, Mr. Mace. But we need to get moving and head for home. Jonah, I'll see you later. I hope you both have a good day." A quick tap on the gas pedal, and the Subaru jutted a few inches forward. It wasn't much, but it was just enough to force Mace to step back away from the car. Then, in a move that belied her usual stolid pace, she gunned the car's engine and sped away.

Well done, Liz. Jonah made a mental note to compliment his mother-in-law for her astute handling of an awkward situation. Then again, she had always been able to smell a phony from a mile away.

But Jonah forced his anger at Mace onto the back burner as he hurried to make it in time for his first class. Today, he had a full schedule right up until three o'clock, when he was hoping to touch base with Carmen to see if she and Kirby had been successful in powering up the phone.

But the answer to that question was resolved sooner than expected when he ran into Sandy in the lunchroom at noon.

"Good news," Sandy called out from the far side of the salad buffet. "I was able to hook your friends up with an old-school power cord when they stopped by last night. I just hope it works on that ancient flip phone. There's a chance the connector might be corrupted after so much time outdoors."

"Thanks, Sandy. I…" Jonah paused, all at once aware of the person directly behind him sending warm puffs of air across his neck.

Mace. Again. The man moved like a panther, his soft-soled shoes sliding silently across the cafeteria floor.

"Greetings again, Mr. Drake. I heard you talking to Sandy about an old phone, and I'm hoping the issue doesn't involve one of our students and some sort of incident in the classroom."

"Not at all. It's something she and I have been working on in our spare time."

Yes, that was vague. But Mace didn't press.

He just turned up his lips in a half smile and seemed to move toward the salad dressing at the end of the counter.

He was almost there when he turned around to grace Jonah with a sly smile. "I'm glad to hear that the faculty is working together for the common good. And what a delight it was to see your wonderful family when they dropped you off at school." His smile thinned. "That daughter of yours! She's quite the chatterbox. She'll tell all your secrets to anyone who will listen. Too bad she took that fall and hurt her leg. You need to teach her to watch her step, lest something more serious should happen in the future."

ELEVEN

Alarm bells sounded in Jonah's brain. The menace in Mace's tone was palpable, and so was the unstated threat in what he had said about Betty. He needed to get his daughter to a safe place—as soon as possible.

Just that quickly, he had an idea that might actually work. Betty's birthday was in three days. He and Elizabeth had made a low-key plan to celebrate with a chocolate cake and a visit to the Duluth Zoo. But what if instead they marked the occasion with a trip to Bemidji, a town famous for its statues of Paul Bunyan and his blue ox, Babe? The impromptu vacation would be a fun getaway—and it would serve an additional purpose of putting some distance between his family and Mace.

And although Jonah couldn't take time off from his investigation, maybe he could at least join them for Betty's big day.

Five minutes later, he had made a reservation for one cabin with two bedrooms and a kitchen for one week, starting today. They would be the only guests on the property, the owner had said on the phone, but they could count on running water and plenty of wood for the fireplace.

His next call was to Elizabeth, who said she was game for the change in plans—with one caveat. Could they postpone the trip for just one day? There was an important meeting she needed to attend at church, and her car would also be in the shop for a couple more days.

He looked at his watch. He had just enough time for one more call.

Carmen answered on the second ring.

"Hi. It's Jonah. Listen. I had a rather unsettling encounter with Mace in the lunchroom this afternoon." He glanced toward the closed door of his empty classroom. In just a few minutes, a couple dozen students would stream in for the last class of the day, so there wasn't much time to explain. "I'd like to get Betty out of town as soon as possible."

"Absolutely. How can I help?"

"As soon as school is over, I'm going to pick up Betty and head up to a cabin in Bemidji. Liz can't join us until tomorrow at the earliest, and her car is in the shop for the next couple of days. Is there any chance you could pick her up in the morning and drive her to the cabin? It's a big ask, especially since it's almost a three-hour ride to get there. And then you'll need to turn around almost immediately and ride home with me."

"Okay," she agreed. "I have night duty tomorrow, but my day is clear. And Bruno is happy as a clam staying with my mom."

That was it then. Short and sweet. Carmen was on board with the plan.

He emailed the administration and requested a personal day. Now all he needed to do was bring Liz up to speed on the new arrangements.

Elizabeth was ready when Carmen arrived at eight the next morning. Stacked inside the hallway were two boxes of food, a battered leather suitcase and a cold pack containing what Elizabeth referred to as "breakfast on the go."

"It's nothing much," the older woman claimed as they loaded the provisions into the car. "Just a couple of apples and egg-and-cheese muffins, a tin of brownies and a thermos of coffee to keep us caffeinated."

Hard to believe it had been such a short time ago that she was introduced to Jonah's family. But it seemed they had become fast friends in a way that was hard to explain. But could she really trust that it was genuine? Or had the intensity of the past few days created an illusion of closeness that didn't exist in reality?

Whatever the reason, something had clearly changed in her perspective. The Carmen of just a few weeks ago would have found an excuse to avoid being trapped for such a long time in a car with a new acquaintance. But here she was, comfortably chatting away with her newfound friend as she headed for the highway, an insulated mug of joe in the cup holder between the seats.

And, as it turned out, making small talk with Elizabeth was easy. During the first hour, they chatted about everything from their favorite foods to Betty's first words as a baby. (*Dada.* She could have predicted that.) As they moved on to discuss life in Foggy Falls, Elizabeth admitted her only frustration was not being able to find a hairdresser as good as her stylist in the Twin Cities.

"It's funny," she said, tucking a loose strand from her gray bob behind her ear. "You wouldn't know it now, but I had a thick head of red hair. When Julie was born, I just assumed she would look like me. But her hair was blond and straight as a poker,"

"Jonah mentioned that Julie was your only child."

"That's true. My husband and I had hoped to have a half dozen kids, at least, but God had a different plan… Julie was such a great kid. Smart. Funny. But most of all, kind. Just like Jonah. Did you know that he gave up an appointment to the Air Force Academy when his brother died, and he took over the responsibility of running the family farm? Then, his parents turned around and sold the place two years later."

Feeling suddenly awkward, Carmen reached for her coffee mug and took a long sip. Elizabeth assumed she was familiar with Jonah's backstory, but that was hardly the case. He hadn't said anything about his brother's death or about his thwarted plan to join the Air Force. But now that she thought about it, it made sense. No wonder he loved flying so much, even if it meant doing so in small, rented planes.

"He likes you," Elizabeth said softly. "More than he realizes. But it would break my heart to see him hurt again, after everything he's been through with what happened to Julie."

Wait. Was Elizabeth implying that there was something more than friendship between her and Jonah? Elizabeth, of all people, ought to understand that neither one of them was looking for a romantic relationship. Jonah had his hands full between his job and raising Betty, and Carmen herself was fully committed to her job and to helping Kirby in any way she could.

Carmen felt like she needed to say something in response. But what?

"It's not like that, Elizabeth," she said at last.

"Maybe not," the older woman said. "But I can hope, can't I? I tend to get ahead of myself with some of my big ideas. It's just that Jonah is such a good man. And I want him to be happy. Sometimes he…" She paused as she reached down and fished through the cooler at her feet. "Sets up these barriers to shut people out. He even did it with me when I came to stay after Julie died. At the time, I thought it was just his way of protecting Julie's memory, but now I'm not so sure. Would you like an egg sandwich, dear? You can have one with or without tomato. And how about an apple as well?"

Carmen sighed with relief. Apparently, that was it for the heavy-duty talk about relationships. "With tomato will be great," she said.

Elizabeth handed her a sandwich and then settled back in her seat. "Did Jonah tell you that Mr. Mace stopped us in the drop-off lane at the school and asked to sign Betty's cast?"

"He said something about an encounter in the lunchroom, but nothing specific."

Elizabeth paused to take a quick breath.

"I didn't read what he wrote until we got home, but I can recite it verbatim. 'Roses are red. Violets are blue. Legs get hurt. And people do, too.'"

Carmen's heart did a double take. "What? Mr. Mace threatened Betty?" Elizabeth slowly nodded her head. "No wonder Jonah was so anxious to get the two of you out of town."

Jonah was waiting on the front steps when Carmen and Elizabeth arrived at the cabin. He stood up and hurried to meet them. "Did you have any problem finding the place? It's a bit off the beaten track, but it will do for a short holiday." He bent over to kiss his mother-in-law's cheek and then shot Carmen a grateful smile. "I hope the ride was uneventful."

"Of course. Carmen is a wonderful driver," Elizabeth said. "And we made great time, once we reached the highway."

A wave of gratitude flashed through him. How terrific was Carmen? She hadn't hesitated for one minute when he asked her to drive with Liz to Bemidji. He needed to thank her properly when he got the chance. Maybe buy her flowers or take her to dinner at a nice restaurant. It would be the least he could do after everything she had done for him.

As they stepped into the cabin, Jonah pointed a finger at the closed door of the room where Betty was sleeping. "She didn't get much rest last night. It was nonstop chatter all the way up here, question after question about everything under the sun. And then she started complaining that her cast hurt and so did her leg. She perked up quite a bit once we stopped to pick up hamburgers and fries to eat in the car, but she was extremely worried that Grandma would not approve."

Elizabeth shrugged sheepishly. "I think I have her brainwashed about fast food."

Jonah laughed and then turned toward Carmen. "Listen. I realize you just got here. But once Betty wakes up, she'll throw a fit if she sees you and then finds out you can't stay. I'm going to head to the car and grab the rest of Liz's gear. And then I'll be ready to go."

Fifteen minutes later, they were on their way back to Foggy Falls, with Jonah behind the wheel of Carmen's Honda.

"Thanks for letting me drive. I've been so

wired that I'm glad to do something constructive, even if all it involves is setting the cruise control. It's a blessing you were able to help us out like this."

"Elizabeth told me what Mace wrote on Betty's cast. Priority one has to be keeping your daughter safe."

"I'm planning to keep you safe as well."

Carmen seemed suddenly shy as she glanced down at the purse she had set on her lap. "Well, thanks for that. But you might need a break since you single-handedly rescued me at least three times already."

"That's why the phone in the book house is so key. I just wish we'd been able to send it to the BCA."

"Jonah…"

"I know. I know. You didn't want to blow my cover, and there was no way Kirby was going to let you hand the phone over to the Foggy Falls Police Department. I get the fact that emotions are running high on the subject. I just think…"

She shook her head. "You need to believe I did the best I could under the circumstances. I'm just glad Sandy was able to locate a charger. But we still need to get hold of the data, if it's even still viable. Apparently, Shane has some ideas about Sara's password. Clint promised to give me a call if they came up with something that works."

Jonah took his eyes off the road for a moment and sneaked a glance at his passenger. "But you know as well as I do that the minute they took Sara's cell out of the book house, the evidence was compromised. I just hope there's something on the phone that can lead us to her killer."

"Me, too." Carmen looked over and smiled at him, and once again he was struck by her calm and unruffled demeanor. Had she always been like this? Or had a transformation come about during her recent return to Foggy Falls?

He'd like to ask her. But he recognized that, although she had already shared little bits of her past, there was still so much that she might consider none of his business. The challenging part—the part that made conversations on the subject decidedly awkward—was that he already knew a lot of her personal history, information he had discovered earlier when he checked her out on the online database of the BCA. Like all the awards she had received as a detective in LA and her work in the community to set up an outreach program to bridge the gap between citizens and the police. He even knew the details of the brutal rape she'd endured as a high-school senior. He'd be interested to learn how she had gotten through that. She professed to be a Christian, so it was likely that she had taken some sort of solace in her faith.

Or maybe not. Maybe she had reacted to the challenges life tossed her way as he had— by pushing God away.

That first year after Julie's death had been a blur of confusion and darkness. Elizabeth deserved all the credit for pulling him back from the abyss, encouraging him to go to church with her and leaving books like *A Grief Observed* on the table by his bed. C. S. Lewis was an amazing apologist for the faith, but it still remained a struggle to fully accept the notion of a good and loving God who allowed bad things to happen in His creation.

He still had a long way to go on his journey. One thing he had learned was to be grateful for each new day.

"So, Jonah." Carmen's voice was tentative as she interrupted his musings. "I did try to talk to Kirby about the drugs they found at the high school. The only thing he was willing to admit to was buying and using, and even with that, he wouldn't give up his source. I can't say for sure that he's not lying, but I did get a sense there's a lot he doesn't know. I'm sorry. I know this is awkward, but he…"

Jonah shook his head. "Don't feel bad, Carmen. He's your brother, and, from my limited encounters with him, he seems like an okay kid."

"He is." Carmen leaned forward in the seat, clearly anxious to make her point. "I know it's no excuse, but he's really had a difficult go of it the past couple of years. Clint hasn't exactly been the best role model, and my mom runs hot and cold with her affections. Maybe things would be different if I hadn't gone away when I did. I suppose it was selfish, but all I could think of back then was finding a way to get out of town. The fact that I would be leaving Kirby to fend for himself was never really on my radar…" Her voice trailed off as her cell trilled from her purse. "I should get that. It could be something about Sara's phone."

Jonah could only hear one side of the conversation, but it was enough to pique his curiosity.

"Right… Great, Clint… That's very interesting… Okay. Call me when you find out more. We're still on the road, still quite a ways from home."

Carmen's eyes were bright with excitement

as she hung up the phone. "I can't believe it.
They managed to unlock Sara's cell. Shane
did a work-around for the password. Clint
says there are a dozen calls to Mace in the
days leading up to Sara's murder. And—get
this—they actually found a video. But it's
partially corrupted, so they're having problems accessing it. Clint's going to call back
when they learn more. Until then, he says we
should sit tight and wait."

Jonah laughed. "That ought to be easy
enough to do since we're stuck here in the
car for the next couple of hours." He paused to
consider his next words carefully. Normally,
he didn't like to open up about what had
happened with his own brother, but maybe
it wouldn't be so bad to share just a little bit
about his story, especially if it would help
Carmen understand that she hadn't caused
Kirby's problems by leaving for LA.

"Before the call came in, you were talking
about Kirby and how you feel responsible for
going away. But that's not on you. Even if
you had stayed in Foggy Falls, he still might
have started taking drugs. It's a tough world
out there for teenagers these days. I guess in
a way, it always has been. At least it was like
that for my brother, Jerrod. He was an addict,
an angry and confused kid, always looking

for a quick fix. I knew he had a problem, but I just assumed he would find a way to solve his issues on his own. But that didn't happen."

Carmen's face crumpled. "I'm sorry for your loss, Jonah. It must have been devastating. Elizabeth mentioned you gave up an appointment to the Air Force Academy to help your folks run the family farm. That had to be hard as well."

"Less for me than for my parents. I don't think they ever got over it. I hardly see them these days. When Julie died, they said all the usual things, but they didn't really reach out in any meaningful way. It's almost as if they've decided to cut themselves off from anything that might hurt them again. I suppose in a way they're just like me."

He pressed his lips together and shook his head. How had he not realized how similar to his parents he really was? Apparently, the apple hadn't fallen far from the tree.

"But you're not like that, Jonah," Carmen said. "You didn't run away. You stuck around to help with the farm. And when your wife died, you rose to the challenge of being a single dad to Betty. Even though we've only known each other for a short time, I can tell that she's your whole life."

"It's easy to be all-in when it comes to

your kid. It's the other stuff that's harder. Since Julie died, I've become more and more closed off, even with people who used to be my friends. I think it was one of the reasons I jumped at the chance for this temporary relocation. It was an opportunity for a reset and, as an added bonus, I'd get to fly planes. Not the most noble aspiration, by any means."

"I think it's pretty noble, deciding to move your family to a new town to catch drug dealers."

Trust Carmen to rewrite his story so he sounded like a hero.

"Maybe." Jonah shrugged.

"Once your folks sold the farm, did you consider reapplying to the Academy?"

"Nah. That part of my life was over. And at that point, I had already enrolled at our local community college. Then I graduated and got married. And then I landed a job at the BCA."

"Was law enforcement always plan B?"

He shook his head. "Not really. The crazy thing is that I always wanted to teach."

"Funny how things work out," Carmen said.

For a couple of minutes, neither one of them spoke, until the silence was shattered by the warble of Carmen's phone.

She snatched it from the spot she had left it

on the dashboard. "Hey, what's up? What?... Oh, wow. This is amazing stuff. Wait. I can't hear you, Clint. The connection is breaking up. We must be in a spot that doesn't get service. Let me fill Jonah in on what's happening, and we'll make a plan on how to proceed."

She ended the call and then turned back toward Jonah. "They managed to open the video. And from what they've been able to retrieve so far, it sounds like Sara recorded it just a short time before she was killed."

TWELVE

The wait for more information seemed interminable. Jonah sneaked a glance at Carmen. Was she as anxious as he was? Judging from the frantic way her fingers kept tapping on the dashboard, he'd have to say yes.

Exactly twelve minutes later, her phone pinged.

She glanced at the screen. "Looks like Clint is sending us a video from Sara's phone."

"Give me a minute to find a place where we can stop and watch it," Jonah said. A quarter mile down the highway, he pulled into a rest area and parked on an overgrown stretch of grass in front of a battered picnic table.

Carmen set the phone on the dash, tilting it at an angle so Jonah could see.

The screen flashed on a red-haired woman with panicked eyes.

"It's Sara," Carmen whispered as the video began to play.

"Hi. It's me. This may seem kind of silly, and if I'm wrong about what's happening, I'll just erase this later and move on. But right now, I'm a little bit scared because I was looking in Max's briefcase for my sunglasses, and I found these." The video panned to a stack of prescriptions in Sara's hand. Then, after a couple of long shots of a gray marble counter, the camera zoomed in for a close-up that showed the scrips were already signed and filled out for oxy. "So, this is really kind of a shock. I mean, I sort of suspected Max was still taking meds for his shoulder, but when I asked him, he said he was done with all that." The screen blinked off, but a moment later, the picture came back into focus.

"But, wow. This is a lot more oxy than one person needs. So, the plan right now is to talk to him about this and ask what he's doing with all of these prescriptions. I hate to say it, but I think it may involve something illegal. What else could it be? I've just seen so many problems with this stuff at the school, and a lot of people are wondering where it's all coming from. I don't know." She shook her head. "It's hard to believe Max could be involved in this. Maybe he'll have a good explanation for what's been going on. But if he does try to shut me out on this, I'm going to tell him that he needs to come clean and talk to the authorities. It sounds logical when I say it. But he really doesn't like being told what to do. That's why I decided to make this video and hide it. Just so there will be a record of what went down."

A line of static obliterated the next few seconds of the audio as the camera panned back to a close-up of Sara's face.

Carmen stared at the image frozen on the screen. "Seeing Sara like that…" Her voice broke. "It's just so hard."

He understood. It was difficult for him to watch, and he hadn't even known Sara.

But what gripped his attention were the allegations that Mace might've had a hand in distributing drugs at the high school. Back then, it had been oxy. Now it was fentanyl. And if it was true then, wasn't it likely that Mace still had a hand in the illegal trade? Which would mean that his investigation and Carmen's cold case were intersecting in a way neither one of them would have expected.

He hazarded a glance at Carmen. Her face was a study of concentration as she seemed to be processing this new information. Did he dare suggest that the BCA take over the case in light of these new revelations?

But Carmen was already two steps ahead of him with a plan.

"Well, now we have a motive for the murder. But it's still going to be a challenge to place Mace at the scene of the crime. He could admit to dealing the oxy but deny being anywhere near the cabin on the day Sara died. And since the evidence has been compromised, it's going to get complicated. You're not going to like this, Jonah, but I think we need to forward this video to Chief Tuttle. I know you don't trust him. But I'm confident he'll do things by the book when it comes to getting an arrest warrant and picking up Mace."

Jonah felt torn. He didn't want to interfere in Carmen's investigation. But he wasn't comfortable tossing the whole thing back to the chief.

"What about this? I call my boss in the Cities and see if we can get the BCA to take charge of the drug part of the case."

"No." Carmen was adamant. "This is Chief Tuttle's jurisdiction. He's the one who supported the reopening of the murder investigation, and he deserves to be the first to have this information." She paused for a moment and considered an alternative. "But I suppose it doesn't need to be either-or. How about we send it to both Chief Tuttle and your boss at the BCA and deal with the logistics? That way we cover both angles. I think you're wrong about the chief, but this way, there will be more than one set of eyes assessing the video."

"Deal," Jonah agreed.

Carmen didn't waste any time forwarding the video to Chief Tuttle. Then she sent it to Jonah, who followed suit with the BCA.

"It will take a couple of hours to authenticate the video and coordinate efforts in planning the next step. I suppose we ought to head for home. We're still an hour and a half away, and you probably want to be at the precinct when this whole thing goes down. Liz mentioned that she packed us some turkey sandwiches in case we didn't want to stop for lunch. I'll grab the food from the back, and then we can be on our way."

"How about we switch drivers while you divvy up the sandwiches?" When he nodded, she set her phone on the console, walked around the car and climbed into the driver's seat.

As she pulled back onto the two-lane road, Jonah fished through the cooler and pulled out a couple of waxed-paper bundles labeled *Turkey With Mayo* and *Turkey Without Mayo*.

He smiled at Liz's attention to detail. "Which would you prefer?" he asked, holding the packets up for Carmen to see.

She laughed. "You choose. I'm good with either."

He handed her the sandwich with mayo, took the other one for himself, and they settled back into companionable silence to eat their lunch.

"Apple?" Jonah asked when Carmen finished eating.

"No, thanks," she said. "Elizabeth packed a hearty breakfast for the ride up to Bemidji, and now here we are, enjoying a homemade lunch. When you asked me to do this, I didn't realize it was going to be a catered event." She laughed again.

Jonah smiled back at her. Really, Carmen had a great laugh, not to mention a smile that lit up her entire face. Not for the first time, he thought about how easy it was to talk to her and how sweet she was with Betty. But how was it possible that a beautiful woman like Carmen didn't have a boyfriend or husband or fiancé?

Maybe she did. She had never mentioned that there was someone special awaiting her eventual return to LA, but then again, why would she? It's not like either of them had ever initiated that sort of conversation. Once Sara's killer was brought to justice, there was a chance she'd let Clint deal with Kirby and hop the next plane back to California to resume her job as a detective in LA.

"Do you think you'll stick around for the trial if the video is authenticated?" he asked, working hard to finesse his most nonchalant tone.

"We'll see. Kirby's still a junior, and I'd like to keep an eye on him, at least until he graduates from high school. And how satisfying will it be to see Mace convicted and sentenced for murder after all these years?"

Another half hour and they would be home. Carmen tapped her fingers against the wheel. After more than five and a half hours on the road, she was ready for a break, and she couldn't stop thinking about what was going on at the station. It had been a long day, and the sky had been dark and threatening for most of the drive. And now, as they made the turn onto the main highway leading to town, the rain had finally started to fall, first as a light smattering of drops but quickly becoming a steady spray against the windshield.

Her eyes darted toward the console. The temperature hovered just above freezing.

One degree colder, and the rain would turn to ice. Anticipating the worst, she flicked on the wipers and then twisted the defrost button on the panel next to the fan.

"There. That's better," she said as the condensation began to clear on the window. "I suppose we should be grateful it's not snow."

"Humph." A disaffected grunt sounded from the passenger seat of the car.

Clearly, Jonah didn't want to talk about the weather.

Or anything else, judging by his silence during the final leg of their journey. That was fine with her, though it was hard to understand what had put him into such a somber mood. Maybe, like her, he didn't like being in a situation this fraught with uncertainty and so out of control.

Jonah's phone chirped. Now that they were getting close to the larger towns around Lake Superior, cell service had improved quite a bit.

Jonah glanced down at his screen.

"It's a text from my boss at BCA," he said. "He talked to Tuttle, and they're going to let the locals take the lead on this. Apparently, it's been verified that Mace is at home, and they're getting ready to head over there and make an arrest."

What? That was fast. Things were unfolding more rapidly than she had anticipated.

Jonah must have thought so, too. "I'd like to be on the scene when it all goes down. I can pull up his address from the faculty list on my phone." He took a moment to find the address. "Here it is—3245 Clover Lane. And…" Another couple of clicks and he had directions. "Once we get to town, we can make a right on the main road, and from there it's a straight shot to Mace's house, which is on a cul-de-sac at the end of the street."

Carmen nodded. She shared Jonah's eagerness. But showing up at the scene with an undercover BCA agent didn't seem like a smart move.

"I'm going to call the chief and find out what's happening."

She touched the call button on the control panel, and the chief's voice boomed through the speakers.

"Carmen! Where are you? Never mind. It's not important. I'm outside Mace's residence, and it's all gone sideways pretty fast. He must have realized what was happening because he didn't waste any time barricading himself in the house with a high-powered rifle and whatever other weapons he has stockpiled inside. At this point, we're not completely sure if he's alone. We ran the plates of the car in the driveway, and there's a chance his cleaning lady might be in there with him."

"A hostage?" Carmen pulled in a deep breath. That took everything up a notch in seriousness.

"Yeah. But like I said, we're still assessing the situation. So far, he has just fired off a few warning shots to keep us at bay. The SWAT team and the hostage negotiators from Duluth are en route, but Mace is stonewalling, demanding to talk to you. But I don't care what he wants. This is best left to the professionals."

"I can be there in ten minutes."

"No," the chief barked. "It's already a circus here." A crack of gunfire echoed through the receiver. "I got to go. One of my officers just got shot in the leg."

The phone cut out.

For the beat of a second, Carmen considered the chief's injunction that she should stay away from the crime scene. But as much as she tended to be a rule follower, there was no way she was going to miss this arrest. It would be all-hands-on-deck with an active shooter and hostage situation, and she wasn't willing to sit this one out.

Her foot pressed down harder on the gas

pedal. They were closing in on the turn toward town, only minutes away from Mace's residence.

She sneaked a glance at Jonah as the speedometer edged up toward seventy.

"At times like this, I'd give anything for a set of flashing lights."

THIRTEEN

Carmen flashed her badge, and the uniform-clad officer shoved aside the wooden barricade blocking access to a two-block stretch of Clover Lane. Up ahead, a half dozen police cruisers, a fire engine and an ambulance formed a blurred tableau of strobe lights flashing red through the downpour, while in the street, officers in Kevlar vests huddled in groups a safe distance from the perimeter. Pulling into the last open space behind a long line of emergency vehicles, Carmen headed toward the makeshift command center to the left of Mace's house.

"It doesn't look like the hostage team is here yet," Carmen said to Jonah, who hurried beside her, matching her pace.

"Yeah. They're hard to miss when they're on the scene." He shot her a lopsided smile. He was looking…okay, she'd admit it…especially handsome, even though his tan parka was soaked through with rain and his curly hair was plastered tightly against his head.

"I can't see Chief Tuttle either, but he must be around somewhere." She tented her hand over her eyes and scanned the scene up ahead. With the pouring rain and all the commotion, it was hard to tell what was going on. In the last two homes they passed along the cul-de-sac, a fluttering of curtains and a movement of shades offered evidence that neighbors were watching, too.

Ssss KaPow! Ssss KaPow!

"Take cover!" Jonah shouted over the din.

Carmen hit the ground under a stand of arborvitae as clouds of thick white smoke permeated the air.

Noxious fumes filled her nostrils and throat.

"Carmen?" Jonah's voice was muffled, though he had to be only a few feet away.

"Yeah," she said, pushing up onto her elbow. "It sounds and smells like smoke grenades."

As she stumbled to her feet, a long arm shot out from the shrubbery, pulling her into a clearing away from the road.

She yanked back from the pressure in an attempt to break free. The viselike grip around her wrist went slack, and she spun around, finally able to face her assailant.

There stood Mr. Mace.

With a .357 Magnum pointed squarely at her chest.

"Let her go." Jonah suddenly appeared, his finger poised on the trigger of his Sig.

"Shut up, Drake. You're not a part of this." Mace's arm twitched as he jerked his gun upward and pressed the muzzle against Carmen's head. "I asked for you, but they told me you couldn't come. I have to tell you something," he mumbled, his voice slurring. "You can't let anyone hurt my sister. Okay? Okay?" With his free hand, he clutched a spot on his shoulder where blood was seeping through his shirt.

"You've been shot," Carmen said. "Let me call for help. There's an ambulance parked out front. They can get you to the hospital in a matter of minutes."

"No hospital," he moaned. "All I want is a promise. A promise that you'll protect my sister."

An unexpected wave of pity swamped Carmen's senses. Despite the cold barrel pressing against her temple, there was something heartbreakingly earnest in the timbre of Mr. Mace's tone. "Talk to me about your sister. Is that her car parked in front of the house?"

"No," he said, his tone suddenly angry. "My sister's not here. She lives in Duluth."

"Okay. I just wanted to know so I can help her. And I will. I promise. You don't have to do this. Just let me make a quick call and…"

The crack of gunfire splintered the air. Mace's body toppled forward, his mouth open and his eyes wide as he landed facedown onto a carpet of soft needles on the ground.

Carmen gasped. This was not the way it was supposed to end.

"We need an ambulance here, stat!" Jonah cried.

Chief Tuttle pushed aside a tangle of branches as he stepped into the clearing, a pistol clutched in the hand hanging down by his side. "I didn't have a choice," he said.

"I know. But I don't think he was going to hurt me, Chief," Carmen said.

"You can't be sure," the chief replied. "But you weren't even wearing a vest." Eyes clouded with distress, he pointed a finger at her, his voice shaking with rage. "Why did you come here anyway? I told you to stay away."

"I thought I could help."

"You…thought…you…could…help," Chief Tuttle sputtered, repeating her words as two paramedics pushed their way onto the scene.

"You could have gotten yourself killed because you thought you could help."

As they lifted Mace's body onto the gurney, Chief Tuttle took control of the situation. "Get a team up to the house immediately and secure any remaining weapons." He reached down and picked up Mace's weapon off the ground. "As for you, Officer Hollis," he said, wagging his finger once more at Carmen. "I'll see you back at the station."

And with that, he turned and stalked away.

Jonah slipped his weapon back into his holster and slung an arm across her shoulders. "Are you okay?"

Not really, but...

"I'm fine." She swallowed the lump that was forming in her throat.

"You sure?" He pulled her closer against his chest.

A pleasurable sigh escaped from her lips. She wasn't sure of anything at the moment, except for the fact that she didn't want Jonah to ever let her go. She pushed aside that thought with a shake of her head. "I think I better do as the chief asked and head to the station."

"Okay. But I'm coming with you. No way am I going to let you face this on your own. Toss me your keys, and I'll get us out of here."

Easier said than done. All the main arteries leading away from Clover Lane were clogged with emergency vehicles. As Jonah circled the block searching for a way out to the main road, Carmen sat stock-still in the passenger seat. She didn't even comment when, at the corner of Main and Forrest, they were passed by three black SUVs. The SWAT team had finally arrived from Duluth—twenty minutes too late.

A moment later, they were out of the traffic, and not long after that, Jonah maneuvered the Honda into an open spot in front of the station.

Lisa Carpenter rushed to meet them at the door.

"Carmen! I've been worried sick. I heard there was a shootout. Is everyone okay?"

Carmen shook her head. "Officer James was shot in the leg. But besides that, the only other casualty was Mace."

Lisa sighed. "I don't get it. Why resist arrest when you're surrounded? Why not live to tell your story and accept whatever punishment comes your way?"

"Mace isn't dead, Lisa," Carmen said. "At least, he was alive when they loaded him into the ambulance." She glanced around the deserted station. Everyone must have rushed to the crime scene, leaving Lisa behind to mind the phones. "Jonah and I are going to head to the breakroom to wait for the chief. If he comes in, will you let him know I'm available when he's ready to talk?"

"Sure." Lisa opened her mouth as if she were going to say something more, but then shut it quickly.

Around the corner from the reception area was an old office that had been converted into a breakroom during the most recent renovation.

Carmen made a beeline across the room and quickly settled back against the plush cushions of a grey sectional.

"Nice little place you've got here," Jonah said, sliding into a spot next to her.

"Thanks. I'm grateful for the company."

"Of course." He nudged her with his elbow and returned her grin. "All for one, and one for all."

"Isn't that the motto of the three musketeers?"

"Sure, but it can be our motto, too."

She forced a wobbly smile. It was above and beyond the call of duty for Jonah to wait with her at the station. He was a good friend, though his presence here seemed rooted in something more than a sense of duty. But she couldn't let herself go there. Not here. Not now.

She looked down at the floor. "This is all such a mess," she said, shaking her head.

Her words hung in the air as a shuffling of footsteps in the hall was followed the clap of a slamming door. And a voice rang out in the squad room, announcing that Max Mace had died in the ambulance on the way to the hospital.

Jonah was half-asleep as he padded down the steps to the kitchen. He got a glass of water from the faucet and pushed back the curtains to let in the first hazy beams of early morning light. Usually, the hours around dawn were his best time to think. But today his brain was fogged with confusion. And last night's fitful sleep had done little to restore his usual sense of well-being.

With Betty and Elizabeth gone, the house felt cold and empty. Loneliness tightened like a knot in his throat. He missed his family and the security of a normal life. But normal didn't seem possible, at least not until he wrapped up this case. So much had happened that it was hard to keep it all straight. And now, in addition to everything else, he was worried about Carmen.

From almost the beginning of the drive back from Bemidji, he had sensed a shift in their relationship, and because of that, he had been off his game. Of course, he was the one who had reached out to Carmen and asked if she would accompany Liz to Bemidji. But now that he thought about it, maybe it had been rash to take advantage of her kind and generous nature. He had intentionally pulled her even deeper into his family's orbit, setting aside his natural cautiousness in order to make certain his daughter was safe.

And, sure, he'd admit that he had been pleased by the thought of having her spend some time with Betty. And even more time with him on the long drive home. But then in the car, he had suddenly felt the guardrails around his heart clicking back into place as he realized their time working together was coming to an end. Carmen had always been so straightforward and honest with him, and he wanted to say something about hoping for a future where they would remain friends, and maybe more than friends, if he was being honest. But try as he might, the words wouldn't come. What could he tell her? That he didn't know what he wanted? That despite all evidence of their growing attachment, he remained unsure about what lay ahead?

But all of these uncertainties got pushed to the back burner once they got the call that Mace had barricaded himself inside his home and was resisting arrest. Given the seriousness of the situation, he didn't even think about those feelings again until the moment when the assistant principal materialized in the smoky din with a gun pointed straight at Carmen.

His heart suddenly took a deep dive in his chest.

He had pulled his own weapon and lined up a shot, carefully calculating the risk to the hostage. But this wasn't just any hostage. This was Carmen. And his heart had clenched as his finger hovered on the trigger.

The anxiety that had felt so tight around his heart had slackened slightly in the aftermath of the shooting. He had resolved to stay with Carmen when she talked to the chief at the station. And not just to provide support, though he was ready to do that as well. But he had expected to be asked to give a statement. After all, hadn't he been a firsthand witness to Mace's attempted escape? But that didn't seem to matter to anyone, at least not at that moment. The chief had ushered Carmen into his office and told him to go home.

Which he had. At that point, it was past

seven. After an Uber ride to his house, he had called to check in on Betty and Elizabeth, but he hadn't been able to get a good connection. Afterward, he had tried repeatedly to reach Carmen on her cell.

She didn't pick up.

As if things couldn't get any more complicated, he had been roused out of bed in the early morning hours by an urgent message from his boss at the BCA. Apparently, a laptop had turned up during an early-morning sweep of Mace's house, purportedly containing information about additional drop sites for the fentanyl. From the preliminary intel, it appeared that Mace had been the kingpin of his own little drug cartel.

Jonah hardly had time to process that news when a knock at the door drove him down the stairs. On his front steps stood Carmen, clutching two cups of coffee and a bag of muffins from the café.

He was glad to see her. But he couldn't help feeling peeved that she hadn't answered a single one of the messages he had left on her phone.

"Jonah. Hi. I've come with a peace offering. I'm so sorry that I didn't get back to you last night, but by the time I finished my interview with the chief, it was late. And I had to go pick up Bruno at my mom's."

He forced a smile, instantly regretting his uncharitable thoughts.

Carmen continued. "And when I got to the trailer, everyone was there, even Shane, and they all had lots of questions. They had heard the rumors of what had happened with Mr. Mace, and they wanted the inside scoop on how it all went down. But before I could tell them, my phone started beeping with an alert from the station. I guess Lisa didn't realize I had been suspended, so I got an all-unit message about suspected arson at Pinewood Camp. No one was hurt because the place was already closed for the season, but eight separate cabins had gone up in flames and..."

"Wait. What?" Jonah felt like his head was spinning. He held up his hand to stop Carmen from saying more. "You got suspended?"

Carmen shrugged. "Pending an investigation."

"What are the charges?"

"Failure to obey orders and follow proper protocol. Not reporting to the command center when arriving at a crime scene. Not wearing a Kevlar vest around an active shooter."

"All bogus." Jonah was having a hard time keeping the ire out of his voice as he thought about what Carmen had said. "You've got to fight this, Carmen. You didn't do anything wrong."

"Yeah," she agreed. "Well, to be fair, some of the claims may be legit. The chief did tell me to stay away from Mace's house. But whatever. Even if I end up getting fired, it's not like I'm out of options. I can always go back to my old job in LA."

Was Carmen serious? He shook his head in disbelief. "But what about Kirby? I thought you wanted to stick around to keep an eye on him during his senior year."

Another shrug. "I do. I don't know, Jonah. This whole thing seems to have come full circle. I came here to help Kirby, and I still want to do that. But there's a chance when this is over, I won't have a job. And I won't have much choice about moving away. I suppose I could take Kirby with me. The change might be good for him, like it was when I moved out West to live with my aunt."

Jonah pulled in a deep breath. So that was that then. Carmen wasn't going to fight her suspension. Which meant that he could officially stop wrestling with those pesky questions about their friendship that kept popping up in his brain.

Friendship? Well, that was one way of describing the rush of joy he experienced whenever Carmen was near. Since Julie's death, he had become a bit of a recluse, focusing whatever energy he had left at the end of the day on Betty. Sure, he still hung out with the guys from work, especially if there was a fishing trip planned over a convenient weekend. But as far as dating went, that had been a no-go. Truthfully, he hadn't met anyone who made him want to change his ways.

Until now.

But none of that mattered since Carmen was on the verge of moving away. Of course, he could always admit that he was starting to have feelings for her and ask her to stay. But—right on cue—he could sense the hesitation creeping into his brain. Was he really ready to open his heart? And would she even be interested in a possible relationship with someone like him?

He glanced down at the threadbare carpet in the foyer. There were lots of memories in that old rug. He thought back to the day he and Julie had picked it out at Crate & Barrel, their first big splurge as a married couple. It had been an impractical—and expensive— choice, but Julie had loved it. So they plunked down the cash and rolled it up, threading it through the back window of their old hatch-back for the short drive home.

All things considered, maybe the way this whole thing was panning out was for the best for both of them. And what about Betty? True, she was fond of Carmen, but she might well balk at any changes to their well-ordered life.

Carmen must have misread the look on his face because her eyes softened as she nodded knowingly. "Don't worry, Jonah. No matter what happens, I won't forget about Mace's sister. You heard him tell me she's living in Duluth. I'm hoping I can reach out to her later today."

Mace's sister? Oh, yeah. Trust Carmen to follow through on a dying man's request.

"I never had any doubt that you would do that, Carmen," Jonah said.

They moved into the living room. A sturdy sort of silence descended as they sipped their coffee and ate the muffins Carmen had brought along to share.

Jonah settled back on the couch and looked up at the ceiling. Today was a day for thinking about Julie. Five years ago, almost to the hour, she had gone into labor with Betty. The memory was as fresh as if it had just happened—the frantic call to the doctor and what felt like hours of pacing and timing contractions until at last they were five minutes apart.

Oh, they did everything right, back then. They had read the books and knew the perfect moment to head for the hospital. And it was during that short drive to Mercy General that Julie had extracted a solemn vow.

"Promise that if anything should happen to me, you won't wallow, and you'll move on."

She knew him well.

And why not, right? He'd been ready to agree to anything in that moment. As far as he was concerned, wallowing was not going to be an issue. Twelve hours later, their sweet daughter was born. *Mom and baby are doing fine*, was his often-repeated mantra when friends called to offer congratulations.

But two days later, on the ride home from the hospital, a drunk driver missed a stop sign and rewrote the fairy-tale ending to their story. And that promise to Julie faded along with a lot of the memories of those early days.

"Still," Carmen said when a few minutes had passed. "I'm certain a lot of new information about both of our cases will come to light in the days ahead."

Ah, so they had moved on to discussing the intricacies and intersections of the ongoing investigation. Safe territory. Well, he had a lot to say about that particular subject. Why get diverted into talking about feelings when there was so much happening with the case?

"I agree. But think about it, Carmen. If Mace killed Sara to keep her from going to the authorities about the prescription drugs, that sort of ruthlessness would be crucial in putting together a much larger operation."

"True," she said. But she didn't sound convinced.

"I'm guessing you haven't heard what happened at the station. The chief is temporarily working a desk while investigators examine the details of the shooting. But a search of Mace's house turned up a computer that contained information about the distribution of fentanyl in the area around the lakes. It was a huge find. Huge enough to require the assistance of the BCA."

"Oh, Jonah." Carmen's grin was quick and warm. "It's just the break you had been hoping for."

"Yeah. But it means I'm headed off to spend the next few days in Twin Cities to help plan our next move."

"Why is that a problem?" Carmen scooted closer and placed her hand on top of his.

Jonah stared down at their clasped hands for a moment, before entwining her fingers with his own. How could Carmen radiate so much kindness and earnestness? It felt like, if he just held on a bit longer, maybe all their complications would disappear. But that was wishful thinking.

He cleared his throat and pulled himself back to reality. "Well, for starters, tomorrow is Betty's birthday, and I had been hoping to join her and Elizabeth in Bemidji."

"Can't they come home now that the danger has passed?"

"They could, I suppose. But I'd rather they stay and enjoy the vacation."

"What about your job at the school?"

"Given the stuff that's turned up on Mace's computer, I'm assuming classes will be cancelled to give the administration time to sort this out."

Carmen nodded. "Well, since I'm unemployed at the moment, how about I drive up for a visit? I could bring along a cake from Margo's. I seem to remember that chocolate is Betty's favorite. And I can even pick up some balloons to add to the festivities."

Unbelievable. After everything Carmen had been through, she was still willing to help him out. "Oh, come on. I can't ask you to do that."

"You didn't ask. I volunteered. I'm thinking I might bring Bruno along for company. It'll be nice to spend some time with him before he moves in with his new owners."

Carmen was making it hard to say no. Her visit—and a cake from Margo's—would go a long way to making tomorrow a special day for Betty. "I guess all I can say is thank you. Not only for this, but for everything. I can't believe that my drug case might be breaking open at last, all because of your tenacity in solving Sara's murder."

She shot him one of her classic kilowatt smiles, "But you were the one who connected the dots between Mr. Mace and the fentanyl flooding the school."

"Maybe so, but Carmen, I..." He felt suddenly tongue-tied as he considered what he wanted to say. "I've never been very good at discussing my feelings. But the time we spent together, on and off the case, has been amazing. You've been amazing." His breath hitched as he looked into her eyes. "It's been a tough couple of years since Julie died. For a while there, I was barely holding on. But, meeting you changed all that, helped me to realize..." His phone trilled, and he reluctantly let go of Carmen's hand to answer. He glanced at the screen. "It's Elizabeth, probably calling about tomorrow."

His mother-in-law's soft voice came on the line. "Jonah, hi. I'm phoning from town since it has been so hard to reach you to discuss Betty's birthday." The phone crackled with fizzy static for a moment before Liz's voice came back on the line. "Jonah? Can you hear me?"

"I can hear you fine. But I've got some bad news. I won't be able to make it up there for the big day. My case seems to be blowing up, and later today I've got to head back to the Cities."

"How will you get there since I have the Subaru?"

"I'll use your car if you don't mind. The garage called last night to tell me it was fixed and to apologize for the delay. One of the mechanics dropped it off and left the keys in the mailbox."

"But…" A crackle of static blocked the rest of Elizabeth's words.

"Sorry, Liz. Our connection seems to be breaking up. Before I lose you altogether, I need you to know that Carmen's here with me now, and thanks to her, I think we've got the birthday covered. She's offered to pick up a cake and some balloons and drive up tomorrow for a visit."

"That will be lovely. Do you think you'll have time when you're in the Cities to stop by the house and remind the renters to cover the rose bushes before winter sets in?"

"Sure. It will be a good opportunity to chat about their lease, especially since my part in this case might be wrapped up by Thanksgiving."

As he ended the call, he glanced over at Carmen. Was it his imagination, or did she suddenly seem deflated. Perhaps she was regretting her offer to spend most of her day on another long ride to and from Bemidji. Or, maybe it was something else entirely. Maybe, like him, she was wondering about her plans for the more distant future.

"Are you sure this won't be too much for you?" he asked. "Driving both ways, and…"

"It's not a problem. I want to do this. It could be my last chance to spend quality time with Elizabeth and Betty."

"What are you talking about? There's still a lot of work to do on the case. And we're not going to lose touch once we stop working together, not after everything we've been through together. One for all, and all for one. Two musketeers, remember?"

"I do," she said.

But it didn't seem like she believed it was true.

FOURTEEN

Carmen shoved the enormous bouquet of helium balloons into the trunk of her car and quickly slammed the lid shut to keep them from escaping. There was something so contradictory and mocking about the cheerful, floating plastic orbs, their bright colors making her mood all the bleaker by comparison.

Preying on her mind was her promise to get in touch with Mace's sister. After a bit of digging the night before, she had discovered that Brenda Mace had been suffering from kidney failure for the past fifteen years and was currently living in a care facility in Duluth. Carmen had tried to make an appointment to meet with her, but she was told that it would take some time for the facility to approve her request.

Thankfully, time was something she had in abundance.

She turned the key in the ignition and

pulled onto the road. Her lips quirked into a glum smile as she glanced at Bruno curled up on the passenger seat. She sure was going to miss him when he went to live with his new owners. It was almost as if the little pup could sense her melancholy mood as he gazed at her with worried eyes.

Bruno's departure wasn't the only event that would leave a golf ball sized hole in her heart. Apparently, Jonah was headed for greener pastures as well. Sure, he claimed they wouldn't lose touch, but she knew better. People often said things they didn't mean and made promises they were quick to forget. And just like that, her offer to drive up north for Betty's birthday began to feel like a huge mistake. Jonah hadn't asked her to do it. So why volunteer? Why willingly rub salt in a wound, rather than make a clean break?

Pushing back the tears that had started to form in the corners of her eyes, she flicked on the radio. Mellow Christian rock filled the air, and she made herself loosen her grip on the steering wheel and ease the tightness in her shoulders.

This was good. This was the right thing to do. Just because she was feeling sad about Bruno and having doubts about Jonah didn't mean she should flake out on Betty and Elizabeth. A three-hour drive was just what she needed. And despite what Jonah had claimed, this might be the last chance she'd have to celebrate Betty's birthday, and she wasn't about to waste it feeling sorry for herself.

As she drove through the countryside, the miles slipped away, and the songs on the radio reminded her of God's enormous mercy and love. For the first time since returning to Foggy Falls, she could allow both her mind and body to relax. And without realizing how or when, gratitude and thankfulness replaced her feelings of loneliness and loss. A bubble of joy swelled up in her chest. It wasn't that she imagined any version of a future that included her as a quasi-member of the Drake household. But a gift had been given to her—the gift of home and belonging, if only for a short time. And maybe that was enough. She wasn't about to squander these new feelings.

With her eyes on the road, she clicked off the radio and then tapped the phone icon on the console touchscreen. She'd give Kirby a call, not to nag or remind him of anything, but just to check in and say hi.

But instead of the familiar sound of a call going through, dead air filled the space.

Right. Jonah had reminded her of the spotty cell service when they spoke the night before.

She had been happy to hear from him, but their give-and-take had been stilted and awkward. And with her recent suspension, they hadn't even been able to discuss the specifics of his case. Was it wrapping up smoothly? Were there any other teachers who had been arrested as part of the drug ring? And what about the others who had been protecting Mace?

It was disconcerting to be out of the loop.

She blew out another sigh. Even though she had tried to downplay her feelings about the suspension, it still stung. While the rational part of her understood that Chief Tuttle had to do something to punish her for ignoring a direct command, handing in her gun and badge had been humiliating.

She began to scan the landmarks along the road, looking for the turn-off to the cabin. She should be close by now. There it was! She cranked the steering wheel and turned into a heavily wooded lot with a half dozen small properties scattered amid the trees. Bruno's ears perked up at the sound of the wheels crunching along the rocky terrain, and he set his paws on the window ledge, excited to see what new adventures lay ahead.

The single parking space in front was open, so she pulled forward. As soon as the Honda came to a stop, the birthday girl hobbled out to meet her.

"Carmen! You're finally here."

"Hi, Betty! Happy birthday!" Carmen said as she stepped out of the car.

"I'm five! I'm five! I'm a big girl now, I'm five!" the little girl sang. "Are you surprised at how well I'm walking with my cast?"

"I am. And I'll tell you what. You go back inside since it is way too cold to be out here without a coat, and I'll be right there!"

Carmen clipped on Bruno's leash and did a quick loop to the back of the cabin, past Jonah's Subaru, which Elizabeth had thoughtfully parked in the rear. She allowed Bruno plenty of time to sniff around the grass and the trees in his new environment, then headed back to get the rest of her stuff from the car.

It was quite a feat to squeeze a dozen balloons, a wrapped gift and a rather large cake box through the door all while being pulled by an excited pup.

"What a wonderful surprise." Elizabeth laughed as she took the box from Carmen's hands and placed it on the top shelf of the refrigerator. Then, with a rainbow of balloons trailing behind them, she led the way to the living room.

Betty wasted no time in modeling her new

backpack. "Daddy gave me this because he says that next year, I'll need it for kindergarten. Don't you like it? It's purple. And this is my new lunchbox. It matches the backpack. And look at my new stuffy. Have you ever seen a rhino like this before? Grandma made it for me. And this is my box of tiny horses, and also my loom."

"Slow down, sweetheart," Elizabeth said. "Carmen's been on the road since early this morning. She probably wants to relax for just a little bit."

"But she came up for my birthday!" Betty pointed out with five-year-old logic. "And I've been waiting and waiting to eat my cake."

"Oh, by the way," Elizabeth said, "Betty found something that she needs to return to you."

At this, Betty stuck her bottom lip out and crossed her arms. "Why can't I keep it? It's my birthday."

"Because it doesn't belong to you, and you know better than to take things that are not yours."

Giant tears filled the little girl's eyes.

"Tell you what." Carmen felt a tug at her heart. "You go get whatever it is you need to give back to me, and then I'll give you your present."

As if a light had suddenly been switched back on, Betty's face transformed. "Okay. I'll be right back," she said as she stumbled out of the room.

"Sorry for her slight petulance." Elizabeth gave a weary sigh. "Between her cast and the birthday, it's been quite an exciting morning. But I'm so glad you came for a visit. It was kind of you to drive such a long way."

"Of course. I'm just wondering, what did Betty take that she needs to return?"

Elizabeth shook her head in disbelief. "When I was unpacking her old backpack, I found a USB shaped like a cat. When I pressed her on it, she said she had 'borrowed it.'" She made air quotes with her fingers. "From the police station."

"Ah. I know just what you're talking about. Lisa Carpenter, our office manager, has been searching for it for days. Apparently it houses all of her treasured pictures and videos of her beloved cats. The way she was going on about it, you would think it was her child that was missing."

"Oh, dear," Elizabeth murmured. "I know how important pictures can be. I'm so sorry Betty took it. I talked to her about tak-ing things that don't belong to her, and she seemed to understand. Maybe you'd better let your friend know that the pictures are found."

Carmen shrugged and pulled out her phone. Normally hard to ruffle, Lisa had been surprisingly upset about the missing USB, so a text to put her mind at ease wouldn't be out of order.

Found your missing USB. I'm away from Foggy Falls at the moment, but I'll give it to you when I return tomorrow.

Carmen deliberately kept her message vague so Betty wouldn't be implicated in the theft. Maybe she'd explain the circumstances when she returned the USB to Lisa tomorrow.

"Here it is! Here it is!" Betty came dancing back into the living room with the USB.

"Okay, then, as promised, a birthday present for a brand new five-year-old!" Carmen tucked the device into her pocket and handed Betty her gift.

The wrappings were off within a matter of seconds. Bruno played with the paper while Betty hopped excitedly around the room. "Ice skates! Thank you! Daddy promised he would take me skating again when we go home, after my cast is off."

Bing.

Carmen's phone sounded, and she discreetly checked the screen.

Thank goodness! :) :) :) I'd love to get the USB back ASAP. I have slight OCD when it comes to my cats.

"Can we have cake for lunch? Please, Grandma." Betty's excited voice brought Carmen back to the moment, and she tucked her phone into her pocket.

After indulging in chocolate ice cream and two slices of cake, the three of them settled down for a lively game of Candy Land.

Before Carmen knew it, over three hours had passed. Betty tried to stifle a large yawn, but there was no hiding the fact that it was time for the little girl's afternoon nap. "Well, thank you for letting me and Bruno crash your birthday party," she said with a smile. "It's really been fun."

Ding-dong.

"Daddy!" Betty made a move toward the door. But Carmen shot out her arm to stop her. She glanced at Elizabeth.

"No one knows you're here, right?"

Elizabeth nodded.

Placing a finger to her lips, Carmen mimed for all three of them to silently sit down on the floor. Bruno followed suit, tucking his head between his front paws.

Carmen crawled over toward the living room window, pushed back a panel of the polka-dot curtain and peeked outside.

Parked in the middle of the lawn was a Foggy Falls squad car.

The one Chief Tuttle drove.

Jonah drummed his fingers against his leg, frustration gnawing at his brain. This was his second debriefing since returning to the Twin Cities yesterday afternoon, and he was getting antsy. The first of the two sessions had been right on point. His boss recognized that while the undercover portion of his assignment was over, the case was still active, at least until all the leads on Max Mace's computer had been run down.

But so far, the data on the computer was turning out to be surprisingly out-of-date. The shipping logs referred to vessels that no longer had permission to dock in Duluth harbor. Two of the captains mentioned in the side notes were retired. Even the accounting log seemed inaccurate. Already there was some talk that the computer itself may have been a decoy, that there must be another laptop with additional sites and numbers that would break open the case.

Normally, he would have mentioned these details to Carmen when he talked to her last night. But the conversation had been so brief that he hadn't had much of a chance.

He had been beyond grateful that Carmen had been willing to spend the day with his family. But lingering in the air were many emotions. Too many words left unsaid. And the bottom line was that no matter how deeply he might care for Carmen, he was not yet ready to act on those feelings. It wouldn't be fair to Carmen. And it wouldn't be fair to Julie. Already the memories of his late wife were becoming less sharp. But they were still ever present. As they should be. How could he possibly contemplate a new relationship when the smallest thing—a rug, a sound—could bring Julie and the life they had shared back into the forefront of his thoughts?

"Special Agent Drake, would you care to share what you're thinking?" Dr. Rosalie Martin, the staff psychiatrist, leaned forward in her chair and waited for his answer.

He drummed his fingers again. "No." Maybe if he kept his answers short, the session would end soon.

It was his boss's fault that he was here in

the first place. Something about a required exit interview after being undercover. He understood that. But the timing was sure inconvenient, given everything else that was going on.

"Well, at the very least, can you tell me why you're being so uncooperative?"

Jonah fought the urge to sigh. "I'm sorry. I know this is your job, but it just seems like a waste of time. At least right now. The case is still active, and I don't see how sitting and talking to you helps anything."

"Well, of course, as far as the case is concerned, talking to me doesn't help anything. You're absolutely right."

Surprise and faint hope stirred in his chest. He pushed his hands against the arms of the easy chair, preparing to stand up. "So we're done? I can go back to work?"

Dr. Martin chuckled. "Not so fast. Our time together isn't about your case. It's about you."

Jonah settled back down. This could take a while.

"You were undercover for several months. That can have long-term effects on family relationships. How are things with your daughter?"

"She's great. As I'm sure you know, she and my mother-in-law traveled with me to Foggy Falls."

"And now that your investigation is nearing the end, are you looking forward to returning to your home in the Twin Cities?"

"Sure." He shrugged. "Why not?"

"Perhaps because you may have formed new attachments while you were undercover on the job."

"Huh?"

"Let's try this another way. Did you work closely with someone while on assignment? Forge a new friendship? Take the first steps in a romantic involvement?"

Jonah narrowed his eyes. Was this a trick question? He was fairly certain the doctor already knew about Carmen. He'd mentioned her in his case notes, and the doctor surely had a copy. Would it be more suspicious not to mention that?

"I had some great coworkers at the school. The science teacher helped me out on a few occasions. And I did end up working closely with one of the local officers."

Dr. Martin glanced down at her notes. "That would be Carmen Hollis, correct?"

"Yeah." So she did know. But how much, he wasn't sure. In any case, he wasn't about to elaborate. Not with a stranger. Talking about Carmen tended to do funny things to his heart.

"Jonah. I'm not trying to make you talk about something that makes you uncomfortable. But I'm sensing some reticence in discussing the life you're leaving behind."

He nodded. "Listen, Doc. I'm a private person. Always have been, and probably always will be. And sure, I'm going to miss some of the people I met in Foggy Falls. But it's all part of the job, right? Some things you need to accept whether you like them or not."

"True." She paused a moment and glanced down at the papers in front of her. "Let's chat for a moment about your friend Carmen. I see here that she knew you were undercover."

"She found out and confronted me with what she knew. Obviously, that's not normal protocol. But she was working on her own case, which overlapped with mine. And she's a cop, so she had already started to suspect that I was employed by some sort of law enforcement agency."

"Your cases overlapped? That seems odd."

Odd was one word for it. *Coincidental* was another. But then nothing about his case had proceeded in the usual way. He had found himself hitting dead end after dead end. In fact, the only real break in the case came after the discovery of Sara Larssen's phone. And then there was the laptop, which had also been uncovered in the course of Carmen's investigation.

"Agent Drake. Do you have anything to share?"

"Huh? Nothing. I'm just thinking about the case." Irritation clawed at his brain. He felt like the germ of a thought was trying to niggle out of his mind.

"You seem frustrated," Dr. Martin stated.

"I am frustrated." Jonah pinched the bridge of his nose. "Frustrated about the case. Frustrated to be here when I could be working. Frustrated that it's not quite panning out the way we thought it would."

"Sometimes things seem one way but are really another," Dr. Martin offered.

What did that even mean?

"Is it possible your frustration actually stems from your reluctance to be done with your undercover assignment?"

"No." It was the laptop that was nagging at him. But in a way, Dr. Martin was right. The laptop had seemed like a potential gold mine, but now was turning out to be nothing more than a decoy.

"And this person who was shot and killed. Max Mace. He was the focus of two separate investigations."

"Right. He…"

Jonah stopped short, stunned by a sudden realization. What if Dr. Martin was right—something seemed one way, but was really another? All the evidence pointed to Max Mace. But wasn't that just a little too convenient that it all came back to the laptop? If it was a decoy, was it possible that Mace was, too?

But then how did it end up in Mace's home?

Jonah's palms turned sweaty, and his heart began to pound.

"I'm sorry," he said to Dr. Martin. "But we'll have to finish this another time. There's something I need to check out."

With two long strides, he was at the door. He pushed it open and ran down the hallway and into the workroom. "Can someone show me the pictures from the Mace crime scene? Particularly the ones taken immediately following the shooting, and then the follow-up ones next."

He sat down at his desk and glanced at his phone. There was a missed call from Bill Tuttle, but that could wait. In a matter of minutes, he had the pictures in hand. He flipped through the photos that he had already reviewed so many times until, finally, he found the one he was looking for.

He grabbed a magnifying glass and peered through the lens.

A feeling of dread coiled in his gut.

Mace's computer had been found inside the inner sleeve of a small carry-on piece of luggage. The working theory was that he had planned on leaving Foggy Falls before the police had surrounded his house. But because it had been so well concealed, the computer hadn't been discovered until the second sweep of the home, hours after dozens of cops had tromped through, confiscated weapons, taken pictures and analyzed the scene. At the time, Jonah had accepted the delay and written it off as sloppiness on the part of the small-time police department. Of course, when the trained professionals from Minneapolis arrived, they had tracked down the item.

But he had been unfair. In fact, the officers at the Foggy Falls crime scene had done their job, as the photo he was looking at proved. It clearly showed the suitcase with all zippers undone. And no professional investigator would bother to unzip a pocket and then not check inside. Which could only mean one thing.

Jonah's heart began to thud in his chest. The pieces were falling into place, but he didn't like the finished puzzle that was being revealed. The only people who had access to the crime scene were police officers. He stared again at the photo, his pulse racing and adrenaline surging through his veins.

He jumped up from his desk and raised his voice excitedly. "Is it possible that we've been deliberately led down the wrong track here? Look at these pictures. They clearly show that the laptop was planted after the first sweep. Someone went to a lot of effort to make sure we knew about Mace's involvement in the drug ring."

Tad, his supervisor, frowned and shook his head. "But wasn't the crime scene secured immediately? How could someone get inside the perp's house to plant the evidence?"

Good question. Then Jonah remembered something Carmen had mentioned about the night of the shooting. Hadn't she said something about officers being called to investigate a case of arson at cabins on the outskirts of town? In a small community like Foggy Falls, with a limited staff already pushed to its limits, wasn't it possible that Mace's home might have been left unguarded sometime during the night?

"I think someone on the inside at the Foggy Falls Police Department slipped into Mace's house and planted that laptop, knowing full well the information was outdated and inaccurate. Which means that somewhere out there is another computer with the real information about contacts and drop sites along the north shore. Whoever did this must have been prepared for this sort of eventuality, and with the walls closing in, they would have to be desperate to deflect attention from what was really going on. Maybe it's the chief of police. Or one of his trusted officers in the department. I don't have a name. But I will if you let me go back to Foggy Falls and investigate."

Tad nodded. "There's a Cessna already gassed and ready to go. It was heading down to Iowa, but the trip was canceled. We can get you up and airborne within the hour."

FIFTEEN

Carmen motioned to Elizabeth and Betty to stay silent and remain still. A cold, clammy sense of dread washed over her skin as her mind raced to consider the possible reasons why Chief Tuttle would be outside the cabin. Of course, she could simply open the door and ask him. Or, to be prudent, they could all remain hidden on the floor, hoping he'd think no one was home. But with her car parked in front, that was only a short-term solution. They could—

"Yoo-hoo. Anyone here?" a woman's voice called from outside.

Surprise and anxiety gripped Carmen's throat as she crept back to where Elizabeth and Betty were crouched under the table. She grabbed her phone.

"Is that—" Betty began.

Carmen nodded.

"Who is it?" Elizabeth's whisper was breathless.

"Lisa Carpenter. She's the receptionist at the police station. But why would she have driven all the way up to Bemidji? She couldn't possibly be that desperate to reclaim her USB."

"It does seem like a long way to come just to pick up a device with some pictures."

Carmen looked at her phone to recheck the text she had sent earlier.

Found your missing USB. I'm away from Foggy Falls at the moment, but I'll give it to you when I return tomorrow.

No mention of where she was. Just a promise to return the device as soon as possible.

She turned her cell over to look at the back and then flipped it to the front again. Her fingers moved quickly to click on her settings, scrolling through all the apps. And there it was.

Unbelievable. No wonder her battery kept draining so fast.

Cydia. A common spyware application.

Anger sparked across her senses.

Someone had been monitoring her cell

phone, listening to conversations, tracking her location, stalking her every move.

Suddenly, it all made sense. When she had lost her cell at the lake, it was Lisa who had replaced it. It would have been easy enough to install the spyware that would track all of Carmen's movements as she worked on Sara's case. But why?

"Carmen! Oh, Carmen!" The still friendly voice sounded through the door. "It's Lisa. Lisa Carpenter."

"I'll be there in a minute, Lisa. I just got out of the shower."

Elizabeth gave Carmen a curious look.

Carmen pulled in a long, deep breath and then pursed her lips to release it in a silent whistle. "Listen, Elizabeth. I'm not a hundred percent sure of what's going on, but I'd like to get you and Betty to a safe place while I figure it out. And at the moment, we have an advantage because Lisa hasn't picked up on the fact that you two are here."

Then she had an idea. Jonah's Subaru was backed up next to the kitchen door. At the time, Elizabeth's polite gesture to allow her guest to take the spot in the front had seemed sweet though unnecessary, but now it could be a lifesaver. Since the plot was on a gentle incline, it ought to be possible to drift in neutral down to the end of the trail. Which meant that Elizabeth and Betty could make their escape without alerting Lisa.

She explained her plan to Elizabeth and then added a final detail. "Once you've circled back to the entrance, drive as fast as you can toward the main road. And as soon as you can get cell service, call 911."

"But aren't you coming with us?" Betty's voice trembled.

"I'm going to stay here and talk to Lisa."

"What about Bruno?" Betty wanted to know.

Carmen looked down at the little pup curled up at her feet. His tail thumped against the floor, and his eyes seemed to search her face imploringly. A lump formed in her throat. "I think it would be best if you took him with you. If that's okay."

Elizabeth nodded. "Of course."

"Is Lisa mad that I took her cat thing?"

"Well, I think she wants it back." Carmen wasn't about to lie. "But I also think you might have helped out your daddy a lot by taking it."

At that, the little girl's face lit up.

A sense of urgency shot through Carmen's veins. She turned toward Elizabeth. "Do you know how to handle a weapon?"

Elizabeth nodded again.

"Good." Carmen unsnapped her holster from under her shirt and handed Elizabeth the Glock she kept as a personal weapon. "You'd better take this as well."

"Don't you think you might need it more than we do?" Now the older woman's voice was starting to shake as well.

Carmen plastered on a smile, hoping she appeared more confident than she felt. "I'd feel better knowing you have it in case you meet some unsavory characters along the way."

"What's unsavory?" Betty asked.

Elizabeth shook her head. "Not now, sweetie."

"Ready to go?" Carmen asked.

"I might have to go to the bathroom," Betty interrupted. "Daddy always reminds me before we get in the car."

"There's no time for that," Elizabeth explained. "Today is special because we have an important mission. You're like that spy we read about the other day."

Betty grinned. "Okay."

Carmen handed Elizabeth Bruno's leash. "I'm so sorry," she whispered.

How could she ever explain to this kind

and lovely woman how remorseful she was to have brought danger to their doorstep?

"Now what are you sorry for?" Elizabeth asked. "The way I see it, we all had a part in this. Betty took the USB drive. I told you to text that woman. I think God placed you here to keep us safe. But I still can't help worrying about you."

Carmen pushed back a tear. Elizabeth's sweet concern touched her heart. "Thank you, but I don't want you to fret. There's a chance Lisa just wants to talk. Maybe a little chat is all we need to sort out this misunderstanding."

It wasn't likely. But this wasn't the time to share her fears with Elizabeth.

Carmen motioned for Elizabeth and Betty to follow her through the kitchen.

"Coast is clear," she whispered, stepping aside to allow Elizabeth to lead the way. Once Betty was strapped into the back seat and Bruno was settled down on the floor, Elizabeth climbed in on the driver's side, and seconds later, the Subaru began drifting slowly down the embankment.

Carmen locked the back door and began to count. By the time she reached one hundred, the car was out of sight, and a sigh of relief escaped her lips. She tiptoed back through the kitchen, stopping by the sink to drop the USB into the disposal before heading back to the front of the cabin.

But as she turned the corner toward the main room, a panicked gasp stuck in her throat.

The window beside the front door had been shattered, and the barrel of a shotgun was pointed at her chest.

"Hello, Carmen. I believe you have something that belongs to me." Lisa stood in the threshold, a pistol holstered at her side. She was dressed from head to toe in black tactical gear, complete with a Kevlar vest.

Gone was the friendly tone she had used when she first came to the door. In its place was a voice that was cold and remote. "Where's my USB?"

Jonah checked his cell phone. He had left a handful of messages, and there was still nothing from Carmen or Elizabeth. Fifteen minutes ago, he had piloted out of the Minneapolis airport in a small Cessna 172. With a clear flight path and stable weather, he'd be landing in Duluth in a little less than an hour.

Still, he couldn't help thinking about Elizabeth and Betty. And Carmen.

Why wasn't she calling him back? Of

course, the cell service was spotty on the more remote parts of the drive between Foggy Falls and Bemidji, but it was well past three o'clock. Carmen should be on her return drive.

He adjusted his hands along the yoke and looked at his location. He was getting close to the midpoint of his flight as—*brrriiinnng*—his cell phone sounded, and he answered with a click. "Special Agent Drake."

"Agent, this is Special Agent Brown from the Duluth office. We've spoken to Chief Tuttle, and he is denying all knowledge of working with the drug syndicate."

"Have you checked his computer?"

"It was clean. But there was a listening device tucked under his desk."

Listening device? That didn't fit with his current theory. "Keep questioning him. And try to find the receiver."

He dialed Carmen's number again.

No answer. He grimaced. He didn't like this. He was now firmly convinced that Mace was just a fall guy. Which meant someone else was calling the shots. Someone connected to the Foggy Falls Police Department. Which put Carmen back in jeopardy. But it was beginning to look like it wasn't Chief Tuttle. So who could it be?

He gritted his teeth. He needed to remain calm and steady.

He tapped his phone again. If Carmen wasn't answering, maybe Elizabeth would.

The sound of ringing echoed in his ear, and he blew out a sigh of relief. This call seemed to be going through. He checked the dials on the plane as he waited for his mother-in-law to pick up.

"Jonah!" Elizabeth's voice sounded muffled, and there was a crackling sound as if the cell service could give way at any moment.

"Elizabeth. Are you okay?"

Static filled his ears.

"Elizabeth. Can you hear me?"

"Betty and I—" *Crackle. Crackle.* "Driving. Carmen still—" *Crackle. Crackle.* "Because Lee—" And then it was just dead air.

Jonah slapped the steering yoke as panic threatened to overwhelm his senses. What had Elizabeth been trying to tell him?

He wished he had greater faith. Faith like Elizabeth's and Carmen's. But even though he believed in God, he knew all too well that bad things happened to good people. And he wasn't particularly interested in having a friendly relationship with an Almighty Being who took away brand-new mothers or allowed a young man to overdose on drugs.

Nope, these days, he put his faith in data and proof. And that was what they needed right now. Information. Evidence. Something to give them a fresh lead.

But even if he didn't have a complete understanding of who or what he was involved with, he could still be proactive. He needed to alert the authorities that Carmen might be in danger at the cabin. He redialed the last incoming number.

"Special Agent Brown."

"Special Agent Drake here. I just spoke to my mother-in-law. The phone call was patchy, but I think there might be something going down at the cabin in Bemidji where my daughter and mother-in-law were staying."

"We can send a unit out. If you hear anything more, let us know. We still haven't tracked down the receiver for the bug found in the chief's office yet, but it can't be far since the bug doesn't have more than a thousand-foot radius."

"Right." This was crucial information. If the receiver was close, it confirmed his suspicion that there was a mole at the police station. His mind was racing when his phone clicked again.

"Agent Brown, I think my mother-in-law

is trying to reach me. I'll connect her so you can hear the information as well."

He tapped his screen to reconfigure into a conference call. "Hi, Elizabeth."

"Oh, praise the Lord, we finally got cell service." Her voice still sounded faraway, but at least he could understand her. "I don't know how much of the last conversation you got before the call dropped."

"Not much. Please tell us everything you know. There is another agent on the call as well."

"Oh." Elizabeth paused for a moment. "Betty and I are fine. We are driving east along US Highway 2. We're still not that far from the cabin. But Carmen's not with us."

"Why? What happened?" A lump of anxiety suddenly lodged in his throat.

"That woman came to the door. That receptionist who works for the police. Lisa something. She told Carmen that she had come to pick up the USB Betty took when she visited the station."

"What?"

His mother-in-law rushed to explain what had happened with Lisa and the USB. And how Carmen had stayed back to give them time to escape.

Jonah pulled in a long breath as he considered this new information. He had suspected there was a mole at the station, but he hadn't even considered that it could be the reception-ist. But Lisa Carpenter had the means and op-portunity. As for motive? Well, money was always very compelling, and the drug busi-ness in Foggy Falls had been booming for well over ten years.

"Liz, you should drive to the nearest po-lice station, and we'll get someone to meet you there as soon as possible. I'm going to change course and head to Bemidji to check in on the situation. We'll get some local of-ficers to head there as well."

"Oh, and Jonah, one more thing." Eliza-beth's voice quavered. "Carmen insisted I take her gun with me when we left. She's unarmed."

SIXTEEN

Carmen wiggled back and forth against the chair, hoping to create enough friction to loosen the duct tape binding her in place.

She could only hope that Lisa didn't notice her attempts to break free.

So far, she hadn't. At least for the moment, she was fully occupied with systematically searching the kitchen for the USB.

Carmen rubbed against the wooden rungs more vigorously. Her wrists burned from the tension, and she gritted her teeth, desperately trying to stem the tears leaking out from the pain.

"Where is it?" Lisa spun around, her eyes dark and furious. Beads of sweat dripped from her brow, and she wiped them away with a swipe of her hand. "I'm getting very tired of this, Carmen. Is it me, or is it hot in here?" She unzipped her Kevlar vest and tossed it on the counter. "I don't suppose I'll be needing that since you forgot to bring along a weapon. What kind of cop are you anyway? Oh, now I remember." Her lips bent into a malicious smile. "A suspended one. And rather than stick around and fight for your job, you ran off to Bemidji."

Carmen blinked rapidly. Lisa's desperate rant was having the opposite effect from what she intended. Rather than riling Carmen up, it was forcing her to remain calm and clear-headed. And to wait for an opportunity to make her escape.

"What's on that thing, anyway?" Carmen wanted to know.

"Never mind that. Just tell me where you hid it!" There was pure hatred emanating from Lisa's eyes. "If you don't, I will kill you. Don't think I won't. I've done it before. Everyone always says it's easier the second time around. Not that it was very difficult the first time. Drowning Sara was a piece of cake."

Carmen's heart thudded as she tried to process this new piece of information. A cold clamminess settled over her body as she realized that the woman standing before her was a ruthless killer. So much for her resolve to remain calm and clearheaded.

But maybe that was okay. She believed God had a plan. She had faith that there was life after death. But that certain knowledge was not enough to prevent the pangs of fear in her gut.

But she had already made her choice.

This was part of the job of being a police officer.

And it was part of being a Christian. To lay down a life for a friend.

Lisa's voice pierced through her thoughts. "I'm starting to lose patience." A cold, sharp object jabbed against her neck as Lisa thrust the Magnum under her chin.

Carmen held her breath, her entire body tensed, waiting. She had no doubt that Lisa would kill her the minute she got her hands on the USB. Her only hope was in delaying the inevitable.

Thud. Pain exploded across her head and down her spine as a whirling darkness rose up behind her eyes. But it wasn't a bullet. Instead, Lisa had whipped her pistol with great force against her temple.

"That's your last warning." Lisa pulled out a chair and sat facing Carmen. "Actually, I brought something along with me that might help change your mind." She reached into the pocket of her pants and pulled out a bottle. "'Fentanyl,'" she read the label out loud. "'To be administered as nasal spray.' This will be enough to kill you. Which seems like fitting punishment for someone who won't admit where she put the USB."

Carmen fought against the desire to pass out, concentrating her swollen eyes on Lisa and trying to ignore the ringing numbness that was throbbing through her head.

"You don't believe me? Maybe you'd take me a little more seriously if you knew that I've been dealing drugs since I was fifteen. Did you really think Mace was smart enough to build an empire?" Lisa made a scoffing sound. "Please. I got him hooked on oxy after he fell and hurt his shoulder. Daddy was his doctor, so that part was easy—stealing a few prescription pads from his office here and there. He never noticed a thing. Of course, that was only the beginning. And my little business was going quite well until that nosy teacher started snooping around."

Carmen let her head loll back as she discreetly began rubbing her ankles against the chair again. Tears poured out of her eyes from the exertion.

She flinched again as Lisa slapped her face with the back of her hand.

More tears. She wished she could stop them. Especially since Lisa seemed to enjoy the sight of her pain.

"I'm a problem solver, Carmen. That's why

I'm so good at my job at the station. And that's why, when Mace called me that night in a panic, telling me that Sara had somehow found out about the drugs, I knew just what to do. But before I could get there, he pushed her and knocked her down. Of course. She shouldn't have been threatening him. She got what she deserved, but then he got all remorseful, especially when he thought about the consequences." Another scoff. "The man was a moron. He didn't kill Sara. He just knocked her out. But I convinced him she was already dead before we drowned her. And that took care of our little problem in one fell swoop."

Lisa paused here. The shadow of a cruel smile played against her lips.

"After that, he was putty in my hands. Especially when I threatened to hurt that precious sister of his. Everything was great, and then you came along. Little Miss Detective, poking and prodding into everyone else's business."

Carmen nodded—anything to stall for time. She was just so close to breaking free. She could feel the tape around her ankles loosening.

"Why didn't you just die at the lake?" Lisa hissed. Her face was only inches away from Carmen's. "Or at the high school? This way is going to be a lot more unpleasant. Have you ever watched someone die of a fentanyl overdose? It isn't pretty. So why don't you make it easy on yourself and tell me where you hid the USB?"

"I won't," Carmen said, tracking her glance toward the sink.

"Ha! Your eyes betray you. Turns out you're not so smart after all." Lisa moved quickly across the room. "I thought I already checked the...of course, the disposal. I should have guessed."

Lisa leaned over and stuck her hand into the sink. She kept up a taunting commentary. "It's in there. I can feel it. But it's lodged in sideways. I can't pull it out. Wait... I can just about reach it with my fingers..."

Carmen squirmed again. The tape released on her right foot. The left was free. She flexed her legs. Her wrists were starting to slide more freely as the threads of the tape separated and stretched. Marshaling a last reserve of force, she yanked her hands free and pushed aside the chair.

She surged to her feet, lunged forward and hit the switch to the disposal.

A grinding whir wailed from the sink as Lisa's screams echoed through the kitchen.

"Agghh!" she cried, desperately trying to extract her hand before it was cut by the blades.

Carmen seized the advantage and took off

running. Halfway to the door, she paused to shrug on the Kevlar vest Lisa had discarded on the counter. She might not have a weapon, but the vest would at least offer her some protection.

Three more yards and she'd be out the front door. She had almost made it when a barrage of gunshots exploded through the air. Panting with exhaustion, she flung herself on the floor as a spray of shotgun pellets pockmarked the wall above her head. Lisa continued firing with more frenzy than purpose. Carmen considered trying to tackle her, but the throbbing in her head was making her see double. And the room was spinning under her feet.

She grabbed the loose string of the birthday balloons, pushed open the door and stumbled down the steps.

What was the plan? Her mind was too numb to think more than one or two steps ahead. She needed to escape. Maybe the balloons could provide cover as she ran toward a nearby shed. If she could get inside, maybe she'd find a four-wheeler with keys in the ignition she could use in her escape. Not likely. And not the best plan, but she only needed to cover less than sixty feet. And her chest was protected by the Kevlar vest.

Pop. Pop. Two balloons exploded in the air.

Lisa's aim was improving.

Carmen's legs felt like they were moving on autopilot. Only thirty more feet to the shed. She zigged to the left and then the right, as another two balloons exploded.

Suddenly, the din of a low-flying aircraft registered in her brain. Could it be Jonah? Wishful thinking. She needed to accept the fact that she was on her own. She picked up her pace and ran toward the shed.

Almost there! She reached the door and released the few remaining balloons as she grasped the handle. Locked. She pulled as hard as she could against the latch, but it didn't budge.

She glanced behind her. Lisa was close and getting closer. She needed a plan—and fast.

But the cold air filling her lungs was making it harder and harder to breathe.

Please, God. Please, God. Help me figure out a way to survive and live another day.

Her fingers groped along the planks of the shed, feeling for any loose boards, anything she could use to gain entry. A window? Maybe she could find a rock to break the glass. Her eyes traced the landscape toward the gentle incline behind the shed leading toward a small, partially frozen pond.

"Oh, Carmen! Oh, Carmen, I'm coming

to kill you!" Lisa taunted over the roar of the low-flying plane passing overhead.

Despair began to drip into her soul, but Carmen swallowed hard, squared her shoulders and continued to search for an entry point to the shed.

And then she saw it. Propped against the wall. A wooden hockey stick.

The handle felt familiar in her grip. She looked around on the ground. Was there a puck anywhere? No. But farther down the slope, near the pond, there was a large rock that fit the bill as a substitute.

She didn't have time to second-guess her actions. Holding the hockey stick in one hand, she moved toward the shoreline. She picked up the rock and set it against the ground. And then looked up.

Lisa was only twenty feet away.

She took aim, swinging the stick back and smashing the stone with all her might. She felt the blade make contact as the air exploded with repeated shotgun blasts.

It was all too much. No longer could her body and her brain hold onto consciousness. A weird kind of pressure slammed against her chest. Her feet gave out from under her, and she collapsed to the ground.

And then there was blackness.

* * *

"No!" Jonah shouted. Fear and anger gripped his senses as gunfire echoed through the air. Carmen's body careened backward and crumpled onto the shore. He was so close. Surely Carmen had heard the plane's engines as he approached for a landing? Why had she risked her life rather than stay hidden behind the shed?

An iciness pumped through his veins. How dare this happen to him again? How dare Lisa Carpenter bring so much evil and suffering to this town? The emotions he had kept in check for the last five years, for the last twenty years, were ready to explode. He had never felt more furious and more helpless at the same time.

And he didn't like knowing that he was not in control.

Bing. A text. Well, that could wait. He turned the nose of the plane around and prepared for landing.

Bing. Bing.

He glanced down at the screen. Three messages, all from Elizabeth.

Safe and sound. Praying for you and Carmen.

The second text was even shorter.

Betty says hi.

His heart tightened as his daughter's sweet face crowded the screen, with a close-up on her crooked smile and pint-size nose. His thumb swiped across the screen to play the attached video.

A high-pitched voice broke through the engine's roar.

"Guess what, Daddy? I was a spy today. Aren't you proud of me?"

Jonah shot one last glance at the screen. How could his heart feel so heavy and yet so relieved at the same time? Betty was okay. Elizabeth was okay.

All thanks to Carmen.

She had been willing to sacrifice her life for his family. Two people she had only known for such a short time. That was what Jesus did. He died on the cross for all sinners. Elizabeth was constantly offering little nuggets of Christian theology to him. But in the past, they had been no more than platitudes that didn't help when the real world reared its ugly head. And now, all of a sudden, they seemed full of truth.

A wide, open field stretched out to the left of the pond where Carmen's body lay crumpled on the shore. Tall grass, now turned golden, shimmered in the sunlight. Not an ideal runway, but not bad either for an impromptu landing. He released the wheels, and as the plane touched the ground, he engaged the brakes and taxied along the bumpy terrain.

He pushed open the door and took off sprinting, dashing past Lisa's prone body, a large rock next to her head. Before anything else, he needed to reach Carmen, even if it was only to hold her one last time.

And then suddenly his foot caught on the exposed root of a tree. His ankle wrenched, and his body flung forward. He rolled twice and lay still for a moment to catch his breath. He pushed himself into a sitting position and rubbed his hands along his face. But when he pulled his fingers back, they were damp. Was he crying?

He hadn't allowed himself to shed any tears since Julie's funeral.

Without realizing what he was doing, Jonah somehow found himself on his knees, head in hands. It was as if he suddenly understood. He wasn't in control. There was evil in the world. Evil he couldn't always stop.

But there was goodness, too.

There was so much he was sorry for. Sorry he hadn't been able to save Carmen. Sorry he hadn't been able to save Julie. But it was so much more than that. He was sorry he had blamed God for all the bad things that had happened in his life.

Because there was always going to be suffering. There was always going to be pain.

But thanks to Jesus, this wasn't the end.

Was this what it took to cause him to believe? Peace bloomed across his heart as he pulled himself up.

His ankle throbbed as he hobbled over to Carmen. How could he ever have questioned that he wanted to be with her, to make her a part of his life? He thought about Julie then, about his fear that, in allowing himself to fall in love again, all the memories of their time together would disappear. But that was such a limited way of thinking. He wasn't being forced to choose between one thing and another. His past would always be a part of the man he had become today.

With that realization, all his usual excuses melted away—guilt about not staying true to Julie, worry about Betty, unwillingness to jump in and take a chance at happiness.

He smoothed the hair away from Carmen's forehead. The sirens were close now. The police would be arriving within minutes to lay claim to the scene. He studied Carmen's face. Her cheek and head were swollen and black-and-blue, as if she had been hit hard with the butt of a gun. But, except for the bleeding at her temple, her body bore no sign at all of a gunshot wound. Then he saw what he had failed to notice in his panic to reach her. She was wearing a Kevlar vest.

Gently, he placed two fingers against her neck.

He felt a pulse. And it was strong.

"Jonah." Carmen's eyelids fluttered, and her voice came out as a whisper. "If you're here to save me, this might be a good time."

He turned his head, just as Lisa staggered to her feet.

Like lightning, his gun was out of its holster and in his hand. He fired once, and Lisa fell to the ground.

"Jonah?" Carmen said again, searching his eyes for reassurance.

"I'm here," he answered. "And I'm not going anywhere."

Carmen frowned as she studied her reflection in the bathroom mirror five days later. The bruising and swelling from the attack had gone down, but there was still a yellowish streak under both of her eyes. And her chest still hurt, especially her upper torso, which had taken most of the hits from the shotgun blast, despite it being blunted by the Kevlar vest. But given the way she looked three days ago, she was heartened by the improvement and more than a little glad to finally be home.

She hadn't heard much from Jonah since he and Betty had visited her at the hospital. Nothing more had been said about his whispered promise that he was "not going anywhere." Back to Minneapolis with Lisa's USB—recovered, bent and scratched, but somehow still intact from the drainpipe of the sink—which had proved to be a treasure trove of up-to-date information, with spreadsheets detailing contraband buyers and sellers, locations and drop sites. Getting Lisa was a big win for Jonah, as were the arrests of a number of the men who had been part of the attack at Carmen's apartment.

But while happy for Jonah's success, she was saddened by the possibility that she might never see him again. Already, she missed his lopsided smile and the sound of his voice. He had been a trusted friend and a good companion, always with the hint that, in a different time and place, he could be something more. But the moment for speaking of such things had passed, and she needed to follow Jonah's example and move on. And to count each new blessing that had come her way.

Starting with her amazing recovery. As

each day passed, she felt stronger and even more ready to face the challenges that lay ahead. So much so that this morning she had planned a short trip to the precinct to thank the chief for lifting her suspension and tell him she was waiting to get the all-clear from the doctors to start work. Being back on the job would be another good thing, she decided as she gingerly pulled a soft T-shirt over her head. Misreading her cue, Bruno bounded over, hoping for a walk. "Not right now, boy." She bent to scratch the tuft of fur behind his ears. "We'll have plenty of time for that in the weeks and months ahead."

She could hardly believe she had finally made the move to adopt Bruno. But it had been an easy call once she had decided to stop tallying all the pros and cons of dog owner-ship and just follow her heart. The hardest part had been disappointing the potential new owners. But the agency had promised to find them another dog as wonderful as Bruno.

Good health. Official adoption of her sweet pup. Both were undisputed positives. So why was she feeling so dejected?

Apparently, following her heart had been an easy call when it came to Bruno. But not so much when it came to the humans in her life.

On the drive to the station, Patti Phillips,

her designated chauffeur, was anxious to fill her in on all the recent news. Chief Tuttle was back at work, cleared of any wrongdoing. And Lisa's workspace remained cordoned off as a crime scene, as more and more evidence had been discovered proving that she had been blackmailing Mace for years to guarantee his compliance. After all the hoopla, the assistant principal turned out to be a rather small player in the grand scheme of things—hardly innocent, but also not the big fish they had originally suspected.

And Carmen had finally succeeded in contacting Mace's sister, Brenda, and the news that her brother had acted in large part under duress had provided a small degree of consolation.

Walking into the station felt like a second homecoming as her fellow officers stood up and clapped and called out their greetings. She acknowledged their kind tribute with a grin as she made her way toward Chief Tuttle's office. The door was partially open, and she stuck her head through the opening.

"Mind if I come in for a quick chat?" she asked.

"Of course," the chief said with a wave of his hand.

As she stepped inside the office, she stopped

short at the sight of Jonah sitting in a chair in front of the desk.

With her heart beating double time in her chest, she sat down next to him.

Chief Tuttle cleared his throat. "Glad to have you back, Carmen. I sure am happy that you were able to make it here today. Now, as you may have heard, Jonah has tendered his resignation with the BCA."

What? A rush of heat spread across her cheeks. How odd that Jonah hadn't sent her a text to share the news.

"But the BCA's loss is our gain," the chief continued. "Jonah wants to finish out the year at the high school, but I have persuaded him to work part-time with us as a liaison with the administration. I was hoping the two of you could join forces on this. There are a number of details still to discuss, and I'd like for you to hit the ground running with a plan. Any comments so far?"

Carmen sneaked a glance at Jonah, who was staring stone-faced straight ahead.

"No," they both answered in unison.

"Good. Now, I'm going to have to run, but you can use my office while I head off for a meeting with the mayor. You have a blank slate here going forward. Just make sure you keep me informed." He stepped out of the office and closed the door.

And just like that, Carmen found herself alone with Jonah for the first time since the rescue.

She offered a tentative smile. "It looks like we're going to be working together again."

Jonah turned to face her and shook his head. "This isn't how I wanted to tell you that we were staying in Foggy Falls."

She stared down at the floor, suddenly shy. "It doesn't matter how I learned about it. I'm just happy about your decision. I missed you."

There. She had said it. But was she brave enough to say even more?

Looking up, she saw that Jonah was standing beside her. He took her hand in his and pulled her upright, and the warmth of his fingers interlaced with hers forced all her fears and loneliness away. Was it really this easy to let go of her concerns and anxieties, to take a leap into happiness with just one single touch?

Jonah wrapped his arms around her and whispered in her ear, "I missed you, too. More than you can know." He released her a little bit so she could look into his face. His eyes shone with happiness, but there was something else there, too. A glimmer of uncertainty flickered. "But before I say anything else, I want to make sure this is for real."

"For real?"

"Me and you. This thing between us."

"No. I mean, yes." Carmen pulled in a long breath. This was all so confusing. The decision not to reach out to Jonah and tell him how she felt had seemed so logical when she was back at her apartment. But now, not so much. As reality set in, her heart felt ready to explode with joy. "I love you, Jonah. That's definitely for real."

"Well, good. Since obviously, I love you, too." He kissed her then, once and then a second time, before pulling back with a smile. "And I suppose we'll just have to see what we can do about all of this, Officer Hollis, since you and I are going to be working together. And since the Drake family has no current plans to leave town."

EPILOGUE

Six Months Later

Carmen hooked Bruno to his leash and headed out of her apartment. After a long, lingering winter, it was lovely to enjoy a warm spring day without worrying about a coat or boots. Not that she was complaining. There was something about cold weather that made her feel rooted and truly alive. The first snow had arrived the week before Thanksgiving and remained on the ground until April. But that just meant the rinks in the parks and on the ponds had remained frozen that much longer.

She had even convinced Kirby to go out on the ice a few times, but skating wasn't his thing, as he told her after their third try. When pressed for what his "thing" was, he had claimed to be still figuring it out. Well, that was fine. The fact that he was even trying was enough.

Kirby wasn't exactly a changed kid since the drug investigation had wrapped up. His lips still curled up in that familiar surly expression whenever he was asked to do something he didn't like. His grades weren't great either, but at least he wasn't failing. Who knew what the next year would bring, but for now he was back living at the trailer on track to graduate next spring.

Working with the staff at the high school had been rewarding. There were still some instances of dealing and using, but Sandy Coltrane, who had replaced Max Mace as assistant principal, had instituted harsher penalties for students caught taking or selling drugs. And justice had finally been found for Sara Larssen. As part of a plea bargain, Lisa Carpenter had given up her overseas suppliers and admitted to her part in Sara's murder.

The past few months had been the happiest of her life, but her joy stemmed from so much more than just her professional achievements. She and her mom would probably never be friends, but at least they had finally made their peace. Lynn Trainor was a hard woman, but Carmen recognized the sacrifices her mom had made for her growing up. Despite vigorous protests from Jonah, Elizabeth had returned to Minneapolis. She claimed she wasn't ready to retire to a small town just yet, but she visited close frequently. And, of course, it was Jonah and Betty that filled her heart the most. At least twice a week, they had dinner together. Their relationship felt solid and on the verge of something serious. Hanging out with the two of them had helped fill the loneliness she had carried her whole life. At last, she was part of a family.

Or at least she hoped she was.

Bruno paused to sniff around the tall grass as she mentally reviewed her last confusing conversation with Jonah.

The trouble had started two weeks ago, when Sandy had cornered her in the grocery store and asked about Jonah's future plans. But when Carmen had pressed him on the subject. he had been vague, causing her to wonder if he had changed his mind about Foggy Falls and was thinking about moving back to the Cities.

Carmen pulled in a deep sigh, then tugged on the leash. If she didn't hustle him along, Bruno would spend the entire walk sniffing one spot. In any case, she would get some answers soon enough since she'd be meeting Jonah in just a few minutes. A walk and dinner, he'd promised. And a talk.

A talk. A shiver of apprehension shot up her

spine, but she shook it off. So far, the Lord had provided a path for healing and happiness, and she had to have faith in His plan.

"Carmen! Bruno!" a voice called from the other side of the street.

Carmen forced her brow to unfurrow as she raised her hand to wave back at Jonah and Betty. At the sound of Jonah's voice, Bruno tugged at the leash, pulling Carmen across the street to join his two friends.

As Betty bent down to pet the squirming pup, Jonah pulled Carmen in close. "I missed you," he whispered in her hair.

Carmen felt her mouth mutter something back, but she was pretty sure it was incomprehensible as a wave of tenderness swamped her.

"We've got a surprise for you!" Betty announced.

Carmen knelt down to give the little girl a hug. "Can you tell me what it is?"

"Nope! Daddy says we have to wait." Betty was practically dancing with delight at her secret.

Carmen stood up and raised an eyebrow at Jonah, who shrugged.

"Can I walk Bruno?" Betty asked.

At Carmen's nod, the leash exchanged hands and the three of them set off along the sidewalk.

"Where are we going?" Carmen asked after two blocks. They weren't headed in the direction of Jonah's rental, but meandering along a residential road a few blocks from the lake.

"I thought it might be nice to have a change of scenery. Have you ever noticed how beautiful some of these old houses are?"

Carmen nodded. She had frequently dreamed of moving into this sort of neighborhood with a house and a yard. Nothing quite as grand as the homes they were passing, but maybe a modest one-and-a-half story cottage where she could have her own room.

"I like this one." Jonah had stopped in front of a driveway leading up to a two-story Victorian.

Carmen did, too. The siding was green, and there were yellow shutters on the windows. And it had a large porch that looked out on a wide front yard bounded on both sides with arborvitae. Yeah, it was a beautiful home. One of those places where normal families lived.

She took another step along the sidewalk when she realized that Jonah was already at the top of the driveway, heading toward the front door. Huh. She was all for admiring old homes, but what Jonah was doing was trespassing.

"Jonah!" she called out. "This is private property."

"It's fine. I know the owners. I want you to meet them."

Was this the surprise?

Fighting off her natural trepidation, she let Jonah lead her inside the house.

In the warm living room, a comfortable, well-worn couch was nestled against the wall, with an easy chair facing the large picture window. And there was something strangely familiar about the fabric.

She laughed. "Jonah, I think your friends have the same furniture as you."

She turned around, prepared to share the joke, but Jonah wasn't standing behind her.

Instead, he was kneeling down beside her, and the tenderness in his eyes made Carmen's heart squeeze in anticipation.

"Carmen." Jonah's voice was soft as he looked up at her. "I sold our old place in Minneapolis and bought this house for us. I love you. You've made me and Betty whole again. You've brought so much joy into our lives, and I can't imagine our lives without you. Will you marry me?"

Carmen could feel tears running down her cheeks as she knelt down and took both of Jonah's hands in her own. "Yes! Of course I'll marry you."

Jonah wrapped his arms around her, and

Carmen pressed her face against his chest. She could feel his heart beating just as rapidly as her own.

"Now, Daddy? Is now the right time?" Betty's high voice interrupted the moment.

Carmen turned to give the girl a watery smile.

"Now's exactly the right time." Jonah's voice wobbled just a bit, too.

Betty walked slowly and carefully over to them, a serious expression on her face. "Carmen, did Daddy ask you to marry him?"

Carmen nodded.

A smile broke out on the little girl's face. "Okay! Then I get to give you this! Daddy said I had to wait in case you said no. But I knew you wouldn't." She pulled a black box from her pocket and handed it to Jonah.

Jonah slipped the ring inside onto Carmen's finger.

She gazed at the solitaire diamond winking back up at her. Her heart was full as Jonah scooped Betty into his arms and then pulled her to her feet, wrapping his free arm around her shoulder.

Thank You, Jesus.

This was her family. She was finally home.

* * * * *

Get 3 FREE REWARDS!

We'll send you 2 FREE Books plus a FREE Mystery Gift.

FREE Value Over **$20**

Both the **Harlequin® Special Edition** and **Harlequin® Heartwarming™** series feature compelling novels filled with stories of love and strength where the bonds of friendship, family and community unite.

Get 3 FREE REWARDS!

We'll send you 2 FREE Books plus a FREE Mystery Gift.

FREE Value Over $20

Both the **Mystery Library** and **Essential Suspense** series feature compelling novels filled with gripping mysteries, edge-of-your-seat thrillers and heart-stopping romantic suspense stories.

YES! Please send me 2 FREE novels from the Mystery Library or Essential Suspense Collection and my FREE Gift (gift is worth about $10 retail). After receiving them, if I don't wish to receive any more books, I can return the shipping statement marked "cancel." If I don't cancel, I will receive 4 brand-new Mystery Library books every month and be billed just $6.74 each in the U.S. or $7.24 each in Canada, a savings of at least 25% off the cover price, or 4 brand-new Essential Suspense books every month and be billed just $7.49 each in the U.S. or $7.74 each in Canada, a savings of at least 17% off the cover price. It's quite a bargain! Shipping and handling is just 50¢ per book in the U.S. and $1.25 per book in Canada.* I understand that accepting the 2 free books and gift places me under no obligation to buy anything. I can always return a shipment and cancel at any time by calling the number below. The free books and gift are mine to keep no matter what I decide.

Choose one: ☐ **Mystery Library**
(414/424 BPA GRPM)
☐ **Essential Suspense**
(191/391 BPA GRPM)
☐ **Or Try Both!**
(414/424 & 191/391 BPA GRRZ)

Name (please print)

Address _____ Apt. #

City _____ State/Province _____ Zip/Postal Code

Email: Please check this box ☐ if you would like to receive newsletters and promotional emails from Harlequin Enterprises ULC and its affiliates. You can unsubscribe anytime.

Mail to the Harlequin Reader Service:
IN U.S.A.: P.O. Box 1341, Buffalo, NY 14240-8531
IN CANADA: P.O. Box 603, Fort Erie, Ontario L2A 5X3

Want to try 2 free books from another series? Call 1-800-873-8635 or visit www.ReaderService.com.

---

*Terms and prices subject to change without notice. Prices do not include sales taxes, which will be charged (if applicable) based on your state or country of residence. Canadian residents will be charged applicable taxes. Offer not valid in Quebec. This offer is limited to one order per household. Books received may not be as shown. Not valid for current subscribers to the Mystery Library or Essential Suspense Collection. All orders subject to approval. Credit or debit balances in a customer's account(s) may be offset by any other outstanding balance owed by or to the customer. Please allow 4 to 6 weeks for delivery. Offer available while quantities last.

Your Privacy—Your information is being collected by Harlequin Enterprises ULC, operating as Harlequin Reader Service. For a complete summary of the information we collect, how we use this information and to whom it is disclosed, please visit our privacy notice located at corporate.harlequin.com/privacy-notice. From time to time we may also exchange your personal information with reputable third parties. If you wish to opt out of this sharing of your personal information, please visit readerservice.com/consumerschoice or call 1-800-873-8635. **Notice to California Residents**—Under California law, you have specific rights to control and access your data. For more information on these rights and how to exercise them, visit corporate.harlequin.com/california-privacy.

MYSSTS23